CW01431473

Honey Cake and Homicide

A Small Town Culinary Cozy Mystery

Maple Lane Cozy Mysteries
Book 8

C. A. Phipps

Honey Cake and Homicide

Wedding singer blues, one deadly kiss, and a cake fatality!

Excited to finally wed her childhood sweetheart, Maddie's plans for the day suddenly take a horrible turn when a body is found in the most unlikely place.

This spectacular whodunnit has Maddie, Big Red, Gran and the groom, aka the sheriff, scrambling for answers when one of the Girlz looks guilty of murder.

Will they find the killer in time for the festivities to go ahead, or is Maddie's perfect day doomed from the start?

If you loved Murder, She Wrote, you'll enjoy this bakers style because Maddie's not taking no for an answer either.

The Maple Lane Mysteries are light, cozy mysteries featuring a quirky cat-loving bakery owner who discovers she's a talented amateur sleuth.

The Maple Lane Cozy Mysteries

Sugar and Sliced - Maple Lane Prequel

Apple Pie and Arsenic

Bagels and Blackmail

Cookies and Chaos

Doughnuts and Disaster

Eclairs and Extortion

Fudge and Frenemies

Gingerbread and Gunshots

Honey Cake and Homicide

Join my mailing list and pick up a free recipe book!

Chapter One

The Maple Falls community center wasn't fancy. Along with worn furniture, it needed painting inside and out. Still, it was good enough for a wedding, Madeline Flynn decided and pushed her heavy blonde braid over one shoulder. The large ginger cat by her feet studied her as if he knew her every thought.

"Not just any wedding—your wedding," his golden eyes seemed to be saying.

Little more than a year ago, she'd never imagined this happening in any venue. After a bad breakup with her last fiancé, getting back with Ethan Tanner, her childhood sweetheart, had not even been close to the table, let alone on it.

Maddie shook herself. Life had a funny way of working out, and right now, she couldn't be any happier. With her bakery closed on Sundays, today proved the perfect opportunity to look around the center as the most likely venue. Though the group she was with had been in the place hundreds of times they'd just finished thoroughly checking each space. Most importantly, the kitchen.

"Are you sure you're happy with having the wedding here?" Sheriff Ethan Tanner, her handsome groom, asked dubiously.

"I truly am. The Girlz and I will make it look nice. I promise." Maddie grinned at her posse of gal pals surrounding them. Affectionately known around town as the Girlz, with the exception of Laura, they had been in each other's lives since school. They were a force to be reckoned with once they'd decided on something and especially if any of them were excited, slighted, or hurt.

"I know what you're all capable of, so I don't doubt it." Ethan shook his head. "Only I don't want you working too hard for our wedding. You should be able to relax and enjoy the day."

Though touched by his thoughtfulness, Maddie laughed. "Oh, I'll enjoy it, but whoever heard of a bride relaxing?"

"I guess there's that." He tapped her nose. "Still, you don't have to handle every detail. Let me help."

"Like that's going to happen." Suzy Barnes, the local school principal, snorted. "Maddie will have lists and a certain way of doing things and you'll stay out of the mix if you value your life."

"I have to agree." Hairdresser, Angeline Broome, nodded. "Let's just hope that everyone behaves themselves, sugar, and we don't wind up in a mystery."

"Shhh!" Maddie begged her Southern belle best friend. "Don't put that out there."

Angel grimaced. "Sorry. The Christmas drama is still etched in my memory and I don't want any of that for you."

Maddie shivered. That particular drama had centered around a wedding and another close friend from Manhattan. Camille's fiancé was murdered right here in Maple

Falls. The couple had planned on getting married at the local resort, which was the preferred venue for most weddings and important events around these parts as it was more upmarket. Sadly, the death ruled the resort out for Maddie, and luckily Ethan agreed. Especially as Camille was not only invited, but part of their wedding party—as were Suzy, Angel, and Laura, Maddie's assistant.

Laura patted the immaculate red bun on the top of her head and waved a hand at the bland room. "I think if we draped plenty of white organza over the walls it will soften everything."

"That's a great idea, and I'm sure Mom has some white screens at the gallery that we can put up to divide the space and hide the restroom doors," Suzy added.

Angel tapped her chin with a long painted nail. "As your gran suggested, let's put Mavis onto the flowers. She does them for the church so she'll know what would be best and therefore most affordable at this time of year."

Taking pity on Ethan who was bouncing on the balls of his feet, Maddie gave him a reassuring smile. "It's okay if you want to leave. We'll be throwing a few ideas around for a while."

Somewhat masking his relief, he at least tried to pretend he'd be happy to stay. "I do have some paperwork to tackle, but only if you're sure you don't need me."

"I'm sure. Unless you have something in particular you'd like to add or request?"

"I wouldn't dream of it." He shrugged. "You know I have no taste except for your food."

"Well said, sugar." Angel winked. "Now off you go and leave us to our plans."

Ethan needed no further encouragement and with a quick peck on Maddie's cheek, he was gone.

"Well, that was painless," Suzy teased. "He's a great sheriff, but not so good on making wedding decisions. The last thing we need is some half-pie gestures of agreement."

"Don't be so harsh," Maddie protested. "He's like a fish out of water with all this. Besides, it means we get to have what we want."

"You mean you'll have what *you* want," Laura noted. "It shouldn't be about us, right?"

Maddie laughed. "When have we ever not made decisions together?"

"I can think of a few instances." Angel ticked off her fingers. "When you insist on getting involved in murder cases. When you run off to solve them without consulting us. When you deliberately put yourself in harm's way."

Maddie put a hand up. "Okay, okay. I get it. But this is different. This is something we can do together and no one gets hurt."

Suzy raised a dark eyebrow. "Can we get that in writing?"

The door opened and in walked her grandmother who everyone in town simply referred to as Gran. She was breathing a little heavily.

"I'm so sorry I'm late. Did I miss anything?"

"Not really." Maddie winked at her friends. "I can catch you up, but it's all just thoughts for now."

Gran stooped to give Big Red a quick pat. "I saw Ethan leaving. Is everything okay?"

Maddie shot a quick glance at the door. "I didn't mention it in front of him, but I spoke to Camille earlier today. She's excited about the wedding and told me not to be silly about booking the resort."

Laura gasped. "Didn't you and Ethan just decide on the community center?"

"We did and there really isn't any alternative, no matter what Camille says," Maddie explained. "It was so kind of her to try to talk me into it, but I'm certain we'd all be thinking about what happened at the resort."

"I agree. It wouldn't be appropriate with poor Camille in the wedding party." Gran brushed her hands together in satisfaction. "Now that it's settled once and for all, we can move on. I know we'll get it looking fantastic for the day. I take it you're keeping the same date?"

"If it's free. I know it's only a few weeks out, but having our hearts set on the resort made it hard to commit until we got our heads around not having the wedding there."

Gran's eyes twinkled. "I happen to know that weekend was blocked out some time back. At least now you'll be able to send out the invitations."

Maddie laughed. Naturally Gran would have things in hand. They had already issued a save the date to all the guests and it seemed that things were going to work out fine. Maddie looked around the room once more and sighed happily. "That's definitely next on my list. Is there anything else we need to look at while we're here?"

"Did you notice that broken pane?" Laura pointed to a side door that opened out into a small patio.

"Ethan mentioned it. Thanks for reminding me. I'm sure they're aware of it, but could you speak to the committee, Gran?"

"Goodness. I wonder how long it's been like that for? We had our meeting last Monday and since then, we've had morning tea on Wednesday. It wasn't broken then. I must check with the other groups that use the center."

"Perhaps Bernie knocked up a stone when he was mowing," Laura suggested.

"Oh, I'm not so concerned with how it happened,"

Gran insisted. "I simply want to ensure that people report any issues so they don't escalate."

"Escalate?"

"A broken window can smash and let in rain or someone could take the opportunity to break in. Not that there's anything in here worth too much, but there are all the things that the groups use, like arts, sports, and exercise equipment, which would be mighty frustrating and expensive to replace."

Gran seemed unusually annoyed and Maddie put an arm around her shoulder. "Then it's lucky we noticed it before any of that happened."

"Lucky indeed."

Maddie wasn't concerned about the window this far out from the wedding and assumed that Gran was merely taking her role on the committee seriously.

"I can't think of anything else and we've ticked off everything on your list to check," Angel declared. "Shall we come to your place to work on the invitations this afternoon?"

"That would be great. Since Ethan's working, we'll have the apartment to ourselves. Gran, would you talk to Mavis about the flowers?"

"I already spoke to her and she's more than happy to organize them once you give her a budget. In fact, being involved has made her about as excited as a dog with a new toy."

"Gran!" Maddie admonished, but they all laughed. Her grandmother's friend was excitable at the best of times.

Everything was falling into place and once the invitations went out, Maddie felt that the wedding would finally happen. After the death of Camille's fiancé, and the worry over the venue, she hadn't felt right about organizing the wedding any earlier. That delay had come back to bite her. However, she was known for her organizational skills that she'd inherited from her English gran and her secret agent grandad. Besides, it wasn't as if she had to do it by herself. The Girlz would make sure of it.

With a lighter heart, she led the group outside to make the short walk to the Maple Lane Bakery with Big Red marching beside her.

Chapter Two

Big Red made sure he got another round of pats in as they settled upstairs in Maddie's apartment over the bakery. Gran sat at the small dining table beside Maddie, who immediately opened a notebook specifically for the wedding.

Suzy snorted. "That's looking full."

"You know she's been in planning mode for months, which naturally means lists, and she's the queen of lists, aren't you, sugar?"

Maddie shrugged, not bothered by Angel's ribbing. "They work for me. Now be quiet and let me run through them with you." Checking everything was designated into tasks that one of them would tackle or they could designate to someone else took a little time.

A while later, Angel looked pointedly at the kitchen counter where Maddie had earlier placed a selection of cakes and slices from the bakery. "Are we nearly done? My stomach is rumbling."

"I'm surprised you lasted this long without food," Suzy teased.

Though Angel was slim like a model, she ate like a teenage boy. It was both fascinating and annoying to witness when Maddie and Suzy had to watch what they ate. Laura was somewhere in the middle and found Angel's love of sweet things troubling. This amused Angel, who loved to tease the serious Laura about it.

Embarrassed at not thinking of it sooner, Maddie jumped up to grab the plates from the counter. "I'm so sorry. I didn't realize how long we've been talking."

"That's okay. This was important," Laura said as she came to help by making a pot of tea while Maddie organized coffee.

Soon they were enjoying the treats and Gran sipped her fresh tea thoughtfully.

"I'm feeling more confident that everything has been addressed on your list. What about you, dear?"

Maddie checked her lists for the wedding. "I'm happy about everything except for one major detail we haven't discussed."

Angel wiped her mouth with a napkin and leaned forward eagerly. "The dress?"

If anyone loved an excuse to dress up, it was Angel, and a wedding dress practically sent her into spasms of excitement. Maddie rolled her eyes. "Yes, there is that, and I promise we'll organize the final fitting together, but what I'm really struggling with is the food."

"It's got to be as good as yours—is that what you mean?" Suzy asked.

"I do want everything to be as perfect as possible," Maddie admitted. "Is that wrong?"

Gran tutted. "Not wrong, dear, but a wedding isn't all about the food. It's about the union of two people and celebrating the day with friends and family."

Maddie nodded slowly. "I hear what you're saying and I wish I didn't have such a hang-up about it."

This time Angel handed her some tough love. "Well, you need to get over it and choose someone fast, sugar, because there is no way you are cooking on your wedding day."

"I get that it would be difficult, but with all the angst over the venue, the caterers I had almost settled on have taken other jobs. We have to accept that getting a good one at this stage is almost impossible and I likely will have to do it myself." Maddie's fingers tapped her thighs, something she did when anxious. "It isn't impossible, and I'd need to do prep work in the days prior, but I'd have to get several servers to make it work."

"Of course, Luke and I would help," Laura assured her, "but I think it would be too much for you."

Angel tutted. "I agree. Suzy and I would pitch in, too, but you'd be exhausted and that's not good for a bride."

"There is someone who could do as good a job as you or, dare I say, even slightly better."

Laura gasped and all eyes turned to Gran.

"Think about it," she said calmly. "Who do you know that could possibly fill your shoes and you'd be more than happy for her to do so?"

Maddie blinked. "You can't mean Lyra St. Claire—the celebrity chef?"

"You've met her, you like her, and she thinks a lot of you, so don't brush the suggestion off by ignoring the obvious." Gran wagged a finger. "Spending time with her made me appreciate how down to earth she is and Lyra would be the first to say she's trying to put all that fuss behind her. Plus, she lives so close. It just makes sense."

"But she's a celebrity. Just because Lyra moved to a

small town doesn't detract from the fact she had her own restaurant in LA and a TV cooking show. Plus, she's still writing cookbooks and running the odd contest."

Gran's mouth pursed. "Still, it wouldn't hurt to ask."

Angel leaned forward and clasped her hands together as if she were begging. "Imagine if she said yes!"

"I don't know." Maddie wavered. "It seems presumptuous to ask. We're not exactly best friends."

"But you are friends," Gran insisted.

Maddie chewed her bottom lip for a while as the Girlz and Gran watched her closely. A hum of excitement surrounded them. Though part of her would love to cater for their guests, deep down she knew it would be too much, so she caved under the pressure. "Okay. I'll ask, but I won't beg."

"No one said anything about begging," Suzy admonished. "Though maybe a little pleading wouldn't hurt."

While she understood they wanted her to have an amazing wedding, Maddie hated to impose, and the celebrity chef wasn't just anyone. Having had her share of problems in the past, with a couple of murders and a stalker, Lyra was also busy running a diner. However, Maddie couldn't deny the thrill of possibility.

Gran stood and took plates to the kitchen. "It's Sunday night. The perfect time to phone her. We'll get out of your hair so you can do it in private."

She loved Gran more than life, but it would be fair to say that her grandmother had manipulated her more than a few times. Still, the septuagenerian was rarely wrong about things. Maddie had said she would do it, and if not now, when? Besides, she'd only stress about making the call until she did.

As soon as the door was closed behind them, Maddie

went back upstairs to locate her phone. Lyra was probably busy at the Beagle Diner and most likely not answering calls.

"Hello?"

Maddie gulped. That was fast and though it was her personal number, Maddie had expected if anyone answered, it would be Lyra's assistant, Maggie—though it was a Sunday. "Lyra? It's Madeline Flynn."

"Yes, I see that. What a nice surprise. It's lovely to hear from you. How is everything going in Maple Falls?"

"The bakery is doing amazing, thanks to winning your competition."

"It was well-deserved and I'm so glad it helped in some way."

"It certainly did." Maddie swallowed hard. "Ah, how are you?"

Lyra laughed. "I think we know each other well enough that we can dispense with more pleasantries. What's up?"

Though she sat in her apartment alone, Maddie's cheeks burned. She really wasn't any good at subterfuge with people she cared about. "I'm getting married in a few weeks."

"Congratulations! From what I saw of your sheriff, I'd say you picked a good guy."

"Thank you. He's awesome."

There was a pause before Lyra replied, "And yet you don't sound too happy about it."

Maddie gasped. "I don't mean to give that impression. I'm so happy. It's just that I urgently need a caterer," she blurted.

There was another awkward pause and Maddie hastened to fill it by explaining how she'd let things slide because of her friend's problems.

13

Lyra tutted. "That's an awful thing to happen, and I completely understand how you wouldn't want to upset her or have those memories taint your special day."

"Thanks and I'm sorry to throw this on you at such short notice. Only, as you can imagine, with the wedding being just a few weeks away and the caterers I had earmarked booking other clients, it's become a huge problem. When Gran suggested you might be able to help in some way, I told her it was too much to ask...." Maddie couldn't continue and instead held her breath.

"Hmmm. My latest cookbook is at the editors, but I am working on my friend Maggie's wedding. Look, if you send me the details and give me some time to think on it, I'll get back to you in a day or two."

The air came out in a rush, making Maddie cough. "That would be awesome and please don't think you have to do anything. I truly understand how precious your time is."

"I know you do, and that's why I'm not saying no outright," Lyra said kindly. "Plus, it could be mutually beneficial as I'm hoping you're still available to help with Maggie's wedding in a couple of months."

While Lyra had mentioned it as part of the reason for the competition, having heard no more, Maddie had almost forgotten about it. "Of course. If you still need me."

"Absolutely! I've been meaning to call you, but life has been hectic since the baking competition last month. The press were back on my tail and I had the cookbook to finish, so Maggie's wedding has also taken a back seat. I'll get back to you very soon, I promise."

As soon as the conversation ended, Maddie phoned Gran, still buzzing. "It sounded promising, but nothing is confirmed and I'm trying not to get my hopes up."

"Lyra won't let you down." Gran was emphatic. "After all, you helped solve that murder in Cozy Hollow for her."

"I did very little," Maddie protested.

"I'm sure she doesn't see it that way. Especially after you won her competition and she's expecting you to help her out with her friend's wedding."

"She did mention that. At the time I was excited about working with Lyra, but I'd begun to think she might have changed her mind and found someone better."

"That's ridiculous. You're more than qualified, and she wouldn't have asked you if she didn't have complete faith in your abilities."

"Thanks, Gran. To be honest, my stomach has butterflies. Firstly with her possibly cooking for the wedding, and now I might be working with her."

Gran laughed. "One thing at a time, dear. It is exciting that she's considering doing the catering. I just hope the press doesn't get wind of it."

"Yes, we should definitely keep this between us. I'd hate for our wedding to turn into a show."

Plus, Ethan would hate it.

Chapter Three

Mondays were always busy at Maple Lane Bakery, especially around the breakfast rush, which began around 6:00 a.m. and didn't stop until the children were at school. Then came the morning tea/coffee groups, which included some moms but were mainly an older set.

Mavis sat at the corner table she and her friends had commandeered as theirs from the day the bakery first opened its doors. On Mavis's left sat Mayor Irene Fitzgibbons. To her right was Nora Beatty. Where Irene was even-tempered, Mavis was a ray of gossipy sunlight, and along with Nora, a dour glass-half-empty woman, they were all firm friends of Gran's.

Right now, Mavis was in full-on mode. "I've given Gran a list of suitable flowers I recommend. I know where I can get my hands on them at the right time. Pick up should be first thing in the morning on the day of the wedding, so we have them ready and they haven't had a chance to wilt."

"Or die," Nora stated. "Flowers don't last long once they're picked."

"Naturally, we'll put them in buckets of water until required." Mavis gave her friend a pointed look.

"Where will you get the buckets from?" Irene asked. "There will be some at the golf club I could borrow on your behalf."

"Thanks, that's a great idea." Maddie smiled as she mentally ticked off another thing. "We can ask around for more if needed. Did you want the usual coffee?"

"Yes, please." Mavis nodded.

"Will there be any free ones for our help?"

"Nora! We're doing this for Gran and Maddie," Mavis chided. "We don't need payment."

"Free coffee and maybe a muffin isn't too much to ask," Nora pressed. "Is it?"

"Of course not," Maddie assured her. At this rate it was going to be a long few weeks and her profit margin was likely to take a hammering.

Nora sat back with a grin of sorts. "You see, asking never hurt anyone."

Mavis shook her head in disgust. "What about music? Were you thinking a band?"

Along with the catering and her dress, this was weighing on Maddie's mind. Everyone had a suggestion and Ethan hadn't liked any of them. It was the one thing she'd handed over to him and he was dragging his feet, which was odd and a little frustrating. "The community center is a bit small for a whole band."

"I'd say so," Nora intoned. "No one wants bleeding ears."

Not wanting to pursue the topic or any other with them, Maddie backed away. "Let me get those coffees." She rolled her eyes at Laura, who was manning the register as well as the coffee machine. Luke Chisholm stood beside her. Their twenty-year-old assistant, who was also in training, made up the orders and delivered them to the customers and cleared tables. The team of three—four when Gran came to help out—was a well-oiled machine.

Up hours before the bakery opened to make bread, muffins, and cookies, and get them into the display cases beside and on the counter, made for long days and she knew she could never do it without her team. Fitting in the wedding organization around running the bakery had been tough. Needing that final fitting for her wedding dress should be next on the list, but she could see that the music situation was turning into an issue.

Absently, she handed Laura the coffee and muffin order and explained it was on the house before escaping into the kitchen. Icing cupcakes might give her some reprieve from her busy mind.

"Is everything okay?" Luke asked when he came in with dirty dishes. "You look worried."

She eyed him for a moment. Luke was obsessed with music and always had something playing softly in the background so as not to disturb the customers. "You don't know of any local musicians, suitable for a wedding, do you?"

"There are a few I've heard of." He tilted his head. "What kind of music are you after?"

"Easy listening. Maybe some '80s music. No rap. Ethan would have a fit."

"So, middle-of-the-road stuff?"

"Sounds about right. The community center isn't huge, so I think even a small group would be too much."

Luke's eyes lit up. "I think I can hook you up with someone. Buddy Preston has a good reputation and he's a great singer, but he shouldn't cost an arm and a leg."

"You've heard him play?"

He nodded. "Several times. He lives in Destiny, but I'm sure he would come down here. Want me to give you his details?'

"That would be great."

"As soon as this rush dies down, I'll get on to it."

Hopeful another thing was ticked off the very long list, Maddie was able to get back into finishing off the cupcakes as well as make a fresh batch of muffins. Once they were in the tall oven, she went over to the desk in the corner, which she laughingly called her office. She didn't mind the open-plan work area but sometimes it was nice to get a little quiet to work on new recipes.

That's why the two-bedroom apartment upstairs was perfect for her. Whether it was going to be suitable for a married couple remained to be seen. She and Ethan had discussed where they would live but hadn't decided one way or the other. She hoped it wasn't going to be too much of an issue. As much as she'd like a proper home one day, this arrangement of being a staircase away from work suited her.

Opting to stay downstairs in case she was needed, Maddie opened her laptop and pulled up the recipe she was working on. It was a honey cake and so far it wasn't quite right. Her plan was to have a three-tiered wedding cake with the honey flavored one to sit at the top of a chocolate cake with a carrot cake at the bottom as this was the heaviest layer.

She hadn't told anyone, but the special third of the cake was an ode to her grandad. He'd given her the present of her first car when she was sixteen, which she'd promptly called Honey, and still owned. The two of them had spent many hours under the hood tinkering, with Maddie learning how to take care of a vehicle. The memories came back every time she drove her. Honey would be the wedding car—if Maddie could decide on who should drive her.

Smiling at the fond memories Honey evoked, she decided to try the recipe again in between rushes and see if adding more honey was the key. Though time-consuming, it was fun to try new things, and this really was a labor of love.

The day got even better when around midday she received a call she'd been hoping for. Her heart beat so fast at the sound of the familiar voice.

"Sorry I didn't call any earlier and I won't beat around the bush. I'm coming to cater the wedding and I'm bringing a couple of friends to assist me so yours don't have to miss out on celebrating with you."

A lump in Maddie's throat made it difficult to get the words out. "Lyra, that's amazing. Luke and Laura will be so grateful, as am I. Actually, I don't know how to thank you."

Laughter tinkled through the phone. "Yes, you do. I'm hoping you'll help with my assistant Maggie's wedding in a couple of months."

"I hadn't forgotten and of course I'll be there."

"I'm counting on it." Lyra laughed again. "I've organized an awesome team, and since I want to enjoy the festivities, I'd like you to take lead on the day, but we'll discuss it all once we have yours sorted. Now, I went over the menu and have a couple of tweaks that will help with service, otherwise it sounds wonderful. In fact, I want to steal an idea or two for Maggie's wedding, so I'm going to pay for the meat as a thank-you."

Maddie was still in shock at her dream coming true and her voice squeaked when she responded, "Steal anything you want, but there's no need to pay for anything."

"I get a great deal from the local farmers here and I really owe you a great deal for helping solve that mystery, and I also have another friend getting married and may need you for that. Call it a wedding present," Lyra insisted.

A few minutes later, Maddie realized there was no point in arguing and when the call ended, she immediately made another.

Ethan's husky voice answered on the first ring. "Good morning, fiancée."

Excitement bubbled out of her. "It's the best morning ever and I have fantastic news. Lyra St. Claire just confirmed as our caterer. Plus, she wants to pay for the meat."

"What? That's amazing. How on earth did you manage that?" He naturally sounded shocked as well as a little reticent.

"We're trading her help at our wedding for my services at the two weddings she's organizing this year."

"I know you're a great baker, but that hardly sounds like a fair trade. The meat will be expensive."

"That's what I said." Maddie told him the rest of the conversation, guessing he felt awkward about anyone paying for anything to do with the wedding, especially a stranger. "When I argued, she laughed and told me it was a done deal and not to worry about it. So I'm not."

"You? Not worry? Please," he scoffed.

She laughed. He knew her so well. "The thing is, I'll worry a lot less with her in charge and this way we both get to enjoy the day."

"Then how can I object?" he said softly.

Maddie closed her eyes for a moment and sighed. Everything was finally coming together and she couldn't be happier.

Chapter Four

Though they were delighted at Lyra confirming the catering of the wedding, it took almost another week before Luke delivered on his promise, by which time Maddie was almost convinced they wouldn't have any music.

"Someone's here to see you," Luke called from the doorway separating the café from the kitchen.

A middle-aged man holding a Stetson and wearing cowboy boots sniffed appreciatively by the oven. When he looked at her, the first thing she noticed was that he had kind eyes.

Grinning proudly, Luke made the introductions. "This is Buddy Preston."

"Thanks so much for stopping by." Maddie held out her hand. "Luke speaks highly of you."

Buddy chuckled. "Well, that's mighty kind of him. He's a great guy and I'd like to help you out, but if I'm honest, getting a request for a wedding is new to me. That's why it took me a bit to get my head around it."

"So you've decided it could be something you'd consider?"

His grin got bigger. "Heck, if it pays the bills, I consider most things. Luke did explain you want something middle of the road, and I have no objections if I can slip in a bit of my own work. It's nothing heavy, just a few cowboy songs that could use a plug."

Maddie liked his honesty. "I'm sure we can work something out. My fiancé and I listened to some of your work last night, and we agreed you have a great voice."

"Thank you, ma'am. The date suits me and if we can agree on my fee, I think we have ourselves a deal."

Laura came by with a tray of dirty plates. When she saw their visitor, she almost dropped them on the counter with a clatter. "Oh my! Buddy Preston!" she managed to say through the hands across her mouth.

He gave a small bow. "The one and only. Don't tell me you're a fan?"

Laura nodded like a bobble-head.

Buddy put a hand to his chest. "This is my lucky day. Have you been to my shows?"

"N-No. I couldn't afford a ticket. But I stood outside the hall in Destiny to hear you once."

"Now that's determination I can admire. Maybe you'd like to come have a drink with me after work. I hear the bar down the street is a good one and I'd like to take a look around—see if they're hiring."

"Me?" she squeaked. "I don't really drink."

"These days I don't much either. We could grab a bite instead. I'd be delighted to have such lovely company and a fan to boot."

Laura gaped for a moment. "I don't know...."

He winked at her. "I may be a musician, but I'm harmless."

"I didn't mean to imply otherwise," Laura stated quickly, then hesitated. "I suppose it would be all right."

"I'll come by at around five if that suits you, Ms.?"

"Laura."

"Alrighty. See you later, Ms. Laura." Buddy went out the back door chuckling.

A little shocked at what just happened, Maddie and Luke waited for Laura to look at them. It took a while and her face was bright red and she seemed just as surprised.

"Do I have a date?" she whispered.

"You sure do," Luke teased. "I sure hope Deputy Jacobs doesn't hear about it."

Laura gulped. "What have I done?"

Rob Jacobs and Laura had been seeing each other for months, but Maddie saw no harm in one dinner. "Calm down. It's just a meal. You can tell him you're spoken for then. Unless you aren't? No one's sure exactly if you and Rob are an item or not."

Chewing her bottom lip for a moment, Laura then nodded. "That's true." Without further explanation, she went back inside the café.

Luke scratched his head. "I don't get those two. Did they have a fight we didn't know about?"

Just as bewildered, Maddie shrugged. "Don't ask me. One minute they're out walking Rob's puppies and making gooey eyes. The next they're acting shy and avoiding each other."

"Love seems to be a tricky business."

She raised an eyebrow at his comment. With his eye on Angel's apprentice at the salon, as far as Maddie was concerned, Luke was almost as guilty of on-off relationship woes as Laura. He looked away hastily and began loading the dishwasher.

She nodded to herself. Love was indeed a tricky business.

The day ticked by and it became apparent by the silly mistakes Laura made that she was becoming increasingly anxious. Maddie sent her to the kitchen to clean up, hoping that would settle her.

An hour later, a distraught Laura dragged Maddie into the corner by her desk. "You have to come with me tonight."

Obviously, menial tasks had done nothing to help. Maddie tried to be sympathetic. "Come with you on your date?"

"Yes, please," Laura begged.

"That's silly. Buddy wants to have a meal with you, not me."

A glint of stubbornness showed itself. "I don't care."

"Look, I understand you're nervous about being with a man you barely know, but you'll be at a bar with other people. If you don't like him or you've had enough of his company, you simply thank him and leave."

"I won't be able to do that. You know how flustered I get. I don't think I'll even be able to talk to him. He's a star."

Maddie had looked up the singer and found out Buddy was well-known, but a star? She chose not to debate that, because she got the impression that Laura was looking for a way to bail on Buddy and she truly thought it would do her friend good to spend time with another man. If it didn't work out with Buddy, maybe it would give Rob the jolt he needed to take the relationship to the next level.

Hands on hips, Laura waited impatiently for an answer and Maddie shrugged. "What if the Girlz and I come and sit at another table? If you want to get away, you can give us a sign and we'll swoop in and rescue you."

Laura considered this. "I guess that could work."

"Good. Then it's all settled. Now, what are you going to wear?"

Eyes wide, panic lit Laura's face again. Knowing that her friend had little money since her parents washed their hands of her, Maddie took her hand.

"Come and have a look at my wardrobe. There's nothing fancy in there, but I'm sure we can find something date-worthy. Luke will manage for five minutes without us."

Chapter Five

O'Malley's Bar, wasn't busy when Maddie, Suzy, and Angel arrived at 5.30 p.m. and took a seat at a table in the middle of the room. It was perfectly positioned to see Buddy and Laura, who sat at a booth in the corner of the room. Laura looked lovely in dress jeans and the long green shirt she'd borrowed from Maddie.

When she saw them arrive, the relief on Laura's face was almost comical.

Angel waved and smiled at the pair. "She's a bit tense, but Laura often is, so I'm not sure it means anything."

"He's nice-looking," Suzy noted. "If you like older men."

"I do." Angel grinned. "By the way he's looking at her, he seems to like Laura a lot."

"What do you think they're talking about? I mean, I hate to be rude, but Laura's not exactly a chatty Cathy, is she?"

Angel chuckled. "No she isn't, but if you meet the right person, conversation can be easy."

"I hope that's the case. Ever since Luke came to work at

the bakery, he and Laura have talked a lot about music. That's got to help on this date." Maddie gave the couple a thoughtful look. "Though I'm also hoping our earnest deputy doesn't decide to turn up."

"Oh yeah. I'd completely forgotten they have a wee thing going." Suzy frowned. "How are the two of them doing?"

"I'd say not so good if she's here with another man." Angel snorted. "One she only just met."

"Well, if Rob's not going to man up and tell her how he feels, then he's a fool."

Maddie shook her head. "Why does it have to always be up to the man to declare his feelings, Suzy?"

"It's just the way it's supposed to be."

"I can't believe you said that. Not when you're always talking about equal rights."

Suzy put her palms up. "Naturally, I'm not talking about you and me or even Angel. But shy women like Laura need a little forcefulness in a man."

Having dealt with forceful men, Maddie felt her stomach clench. "I can't agree with you on that, but that's the least of Laura's problems. Look who just walked in."

Rob came toward their table with a friendly smile. "Evening all. I'd say it's ladies' night at this table, but where's Laura?"

"Ah. She didn't come with us," Maddie managed.

He frowned, and that's when they heard a familiar laugh. All of them turned to the table where Laura sat across from Buddy Preston. The singer tapped his bottle of beer against Laura's wineglass and the couple laughed again.

Maddie watched Rob's face drain of color. This wasn't good. "They just met today, and Buddy was at a loose end so he asked Laura to join him for a drink. He's going to be our entertainment for the wedding," she blurted.

Rob's eyes narrowed. "Well, I see no reason to disturb them when they're obviously enjoying themselves." With a brisk nod, he marched out of the bar.

"Oh dear." Angel blew out a long breath. "I wanted to say something encouraging, but I suspect he wasn't in the mood to be mollified."

Suzy tucked back a curl. "Laura does seem to be having a great time and she's not at all awkward the way she usually is. That's got to smart."

"Poor Rob." Maddie sighed. "I'd hoped that someone else being interested in Laura might push their relationship forward, but with Rob leaving in a huff, I'm not so sure."

"You would have thought he'd at least go talk to them." Suzy shrugged. "You know, introduce himself and show that he had an interest in Laura that didn't revolve around the puppies."

Angel chewed a fingernail. "I feel like we should say something, but I'm not willing to spoil Laura's night."

Maddie nodded. She wasn't sure if Laura being unaware that Rob had seen her was a good thing or not and had to agree that the couple looked to be having fun.

The bar filled up and plenty of people came by to speak to the women, including a couple of local single men. They talked a good game, but Suzy and Angel smiled sweetly and made it known they weren't interested in extending their group tonight. When Laura and Buddy ordered food, the rest of the Girlz did the same.

Another hour passed, and when it appeared that the couple weren't in a hurry to leave, Maddie yawned. "I don't know about you two, but I've had enough and I still have to work tomorrow. Laura clearly doesn't need an intervention, so I suggest we leave them to it."

"Sounds good to me," Angel agreed. "They're enjoying each other's company, and frankly, I don't think Laura cares whether we're here or not."

"Who knows, Buddy might be a better fit for Laura." Suzy gave a wry grin. "Although, I thought Rob was pretty perfect for her."

"Sometimes friendship is all there is. That might be okay for others, but I think Laura deserves more." Angel winked. "We all do."

Suzy rolled her eyes. "Let me know if any halfway decent and eligible men turn up in town."

Maddie laughed. "Apart from you two scaring off any would-be suitors, if they did persevere, you'd still make them walk through hoops."

"I can't help it if I'm particular." Suzy sniffed.

Angel studied her perfect nails. "If it doesn't work out with Laura and Buddy, I'll let him know you're interested."

"You will not! I'll find my own man when I'm ready."

"Sheesh, keep your hair on. I was teasing." Angel winked. "Kind of."

Suzy wagged a finger. "Behave yourself or I warn you, I'll pay you back good."

Maddie didn't doubt the pocket rocket would get even if necessary, though she doubted it would ever come to that. The two women loved to rile each other, but it was all good-natured.

They finished their drinks and with a wave to Laura, who waved back, they left the bar. Heading up Main Street, the group almost barreled into a man who appeared at the corner. Stetson low over his face he hurriedly turned away and went back into the alley.

"Well, how rude," Suzy retorted as the man disappeared into the shadows.

Angel laughed. "He's probably had one too many and just realized he was going the wrong way home."

Maddie tried to ignore the tingle that usually meant something was wrong. The awkward situation with Rob was probably responsible. Thinking that, she tried to enjoy the evening stroll back to the bakery. The other two chattered on about the odd love triangle until they saw Angel to her door.

Bernie Davis, the local taxi driver, waited outside the bakery for Suzy, who'd wisely decided not to drive before they set out so she could have a drink. Big Red waited at the back door for Maddie to say goodbye, and when Bernie's car disappeared around the corner, they went inside.

"What have you been up to?"

The Maine coon eyed her and stalked up the stairs. She knew he would have cruised the streets while she was away and possibly stopped by the bar to check on her. What he actually did, she'd likely never know, but he was always at home waiting for her, as if they had some connection that alerted him.

Maddie might have once laughed at her vivid imagination, except it had been proven time and again, when he turned up at the right time. Big Red had been instrumental in helping her solve several mysteries, and they would do anything to protect each other.

Her skin tingled again.

Chapter Six

Maddie got most of her supplies delivered. With limited space, she grew tomatoes and herbs in the garden outside the back door as well as several fruit trees, while Gran's small farm at the end of Maple Lane supplied most of her vegetables. Along with a couple of sheep and cows, Gran also kept chickens, which meant they had fresh eggs for most of their baking.

Neither of them could kill an animal but, as luck would have it, the end shop in the block of four was a butcher's shop. Thomas Calder took care of that side of things. When Maddie was small, Gran had explained about the circle of life on a farm, so they weren't exactly squeamish, but loving animals the way they did meant they always made themselves scarce when it was time for Thomas to cull one.

He had done so on Friday, and this Monday morning it was time to collect the dressed meat. Or at least a small portion of it. The rest Thomas would deliver to Gran's after work, where there was a large freezer in the garage next to the cottage.

Big Red recognized the bag she carried this morning

was for the purpose of picking up the meat for the week, so he was stuck to her side like glue for the short walk.

"It's not like you haven't had breakfast, or that Thomas is going to feed you," she told him.

Big Red ignored her, and her suspicions solidified that the butcher was likely giving Big Red tidbits, as were the other store owners from this block and probably half the town. No matter what she said, and regardless of his size, people couldn't resist the Maine coon's pleading looks.

They could have walked up Main Street, but she chose to go out the back door and up Maple Lane where the leafy oaks on the other side of the road led to Gran's cottage. Once she got to the end of the block, she would walk around to the butcher's front door.

Maddie got as far as the edge of the small wall that ran along the back of all four gardens and stopped midstride. A cap sat outside the gate. In all the years she had known the butcher, Thomas Calder had never worn a hat. Not even in winter.

She decided to take it to him and see if he knew of anyone who wore one like this. As soon as she touched it, Maddie recoiled at the sticky feel, and her stomach twisted. Checking her fingers she saw the tell-tale red. Blood.

With a jerky step forward, she peered over the wall. Unlike the three other gardens, Thomas's was unkempt. At first, she saw only weeds and the overgrown hedge. It was pure instinct that made her gingerly open the gate and walk up the path. Blood stains on the two steps to the back door had been wiped, but not well enough. She leaned toward the door and saw a small smudge that could have been a fingerprint.

Her mind whirred as she tried to think of a plausible scenario. Accidents happened every day. Thomas might have cut himself or the blood could be from an animal he had freshly butchered. Except, Thomas knew his way around knives, and he was proud of his skills and lack of injury. Also, while he might not keep a tidy garden, his shop was spotless and meat never came through the back door.

Shaking her head, Maddie backed away. There was little point in worrying about what had occurred here until she'd spoken to Thomas. After hurrying around the street to the front of the store as she'd planned instead of simply knocking on the back door, she saw Thomas through his store window. Immediately, she released a shaky breath.

He caught her staring and waved her in. "You look a bit pale this morning. Is everything all right?"

She nodded, licked her dry lips, and held the cap out to him by the very edge. "I'm so glad you're okay. I found this just outside your gate. Does it look familiar?"

He shook his head. "It's not mine. I'm hot-blooded, and unless I have one attached to a jacket in winter, I can't be bothered with them."

She nodded. "I feel the same way."

"You seem upset, and I know you hate unsolved mysteries, but why would there be something wrong with me just because you found a hat?" he teased. "You're more than welcome to leave it on the counter in case anyone comes looking for it."

"I don't think that's a good idea." She showed him the sticky patch. "Did you happen to cut yourself last night or today?"

He glanced down at his fingers, then shook his stocky frame. "Nope. It's a rare day when I do. Besides, like I said, that ain't my cap."

Maddie tapped a thigh with her other hand. "I believe

you. Only, I went inside your gate and found blood on the steps and the back door."

"Blood? That's crazy. I'm very particular with things like that. Besides, all carcasses are brought in through the front door because it's bigger."

"That's what I thought." She tilted her head. "What do you do with them when you bring them inside?"

"Everything goes into the chiller immediately."

"So you don't cut any meat up right away?"

"Never. Even if I have an urgent order, I put everything inside to make sure it stays at the right temperature until I'm ready. When I'm done, I only bring out the meat I need to work on."

"Sorry to keep on about this, but have you had anyone come knocking at your back door recently?"

He shook his head. "I'm up early so I'm in bed early. I will admit that I'm a sound sleeper so someone could have knocked and I simply didn't hear them."

"Well, that's definitely a possibility." Maddie's fingers tapped some more. "If it wasn't for the blood, I'd say not to worry, but maybe we should check around the area in case someone's hurt."

"I don't mind helping, but if you think there's something suspicious going on, why don't you give the sheriff a call? Digging into a mystery for fun is one thing, but Ethan might know if someone is missing or got hurt."

Everyone in town knew that Maddie had been involved in more than her fair share of mysteries, and to be fair, Thomas made sense. If it transpired that someone was missing, then perhaps that smear on the back door was a fingerprint, which might help track the person down. "You're right and it could save time. I'd hate to think of someone wandering around Maple Falls injured."

Thomas frowned. "You're really serious about all this, aren't you?"

Maddie shifted awkwardly. "I know how it sounds, but I have a bit of a sixth sense about these things."

"Sheesh. You just gave me the creeps. I've heard about your, ah, talents, but I kinda hope you're wrong."

Maddie couldn't have agreed more. The last thing she needed was more trouble, but the feeling persisted and there was nothing she could do about it, other than find out what it meant.

Chapter Seven

Ethan was at the butchery in less than ten minutes. He nodded several times as Maddie explained what she knew and handed him the cap. He looked it over, studied the blood for a moment, then whipped out a plastic bag from one of his many pockets and sealed the cap inside. "Do you have anything to add, Thomas?"

The butcher blinked rapidly "Me? Hey, I don't know anything about it. Like I keep telling Maddie, the cap's not mine, and she warned me not to go near the evidence, so..."

"Evidence?" He frowned at her. "That remains to be seen. How about I take a look before anyone jumps to conclusions?"

Maddie accepted the censure since Ethan was doing his job and followed him to the back door via the kitchen. She almost ran into his back when Ethan stopped dead a foot in front of the door.

"Thomas!"

The butcher came running. "What now?"

"Did you come in the back or the front door this morning?"

"Neither. Delivery was Friday."

"Thought so." Ethan pointed at the back door. "Looks like you had a break-in."

"Really?" Thomas peered at the splintered broken lock. "I keep the register cash upstairs in my apartment and that was still here this morning. What else could they take except meat?"

Ethan wrote in his notebook. "Did you check the chiller?"

"Check the meat? Why would I do that when I had no idea about a break-in?"

Ethan's nostrils flared. "In case that's what they were after. I'd appreciate it if you'd take a look to see if anything is missing."

Thomas huffed, the break-in obviously upsetting him. "Fine. Though I didn't see any gaps when I went in earlier." He marched over to the walk-in chiller room and opened the steel door.

A blast of cold air hit them and Maddie shivered. To one side of the room, sides of beef hung from hooks attached to a rail. On the left, shelves held different hunks of various meats waiting to be sliced into salable cuts.

Maddie followed the men down the row of beef until they got to the lamb and pork hanging from another rail.

Thomas breathed deeply and shrugged. "It all looks good to me."

"Perhaps the burglar was too nervous to go upstairs and when he realized there wasn't anything of cash value down here, they didn't bother with the meat."

Ethan's explanation seemed to fit and it was so cold in the chiller that Maddie was ready to leave when something caught her eye. Her stomach swirled in a familiar way and she swallowed hard. "Ethan—is that a shoe?"

He followed her pointed finger to the floor in the corner, then rushed over to it. Pushing half a pig away from the area, they found a man seated there, leaning against the wall. His lashes were stuck together, eyes wide, as if surprised by his predicament.

"What is it?" Thomas leaned over them. "What the heck! Who is that?"

Despite the cold, sweat broke out on her forehead. Unfortunately, Maddie knew exactly who it was, and her heart sank even further as her fingers tapped on her thigh. "That happens to be our wedding singer."

Ethan had checked for a pulse, which wasn't necessary if Buddy's blue lips and bulging eyes were taken into account. Now, he slowly turned his head to stare at her, his eyes flicking to her fingers. "You're sure."

"I wish I wasn't, but it's Buddy Preston, all right. I met him in person on Friday, and he was at the bar that night with Laura."

It was Ethan's turn to be wide-eyed. "Laura had a date with this guy? What about Rob?"

Taken aback by his tone, Maddie rallied to Laura's defense. "There's no need to look so horrified. Until they make their relationship official, she can date who she likes."

Ethan blinked as if he couldn't figure out if she was serious. "Let's concentrate on what time the date finished."

Maddie gaped. The question was nearly as horrifying as finding the body. "Surely you don't suspect Laura of killing Buddy?"

He shifted awkwardly. "You know I have to ask the question."

Maddie shrugged, irrationally irritated by his common

sense. "The Girlz and I left before Laura, so I don't know what time the date ended. What do you think he died of?"

"No you don't. We are not discussing this any further. Plus, my hands are too frozen to work my radio. Let's get out of here."

Well used to the cold, Thomas was pale and nodding profusely. "I don't want to look at him any more either."

Back in the store, with the door to the chiller shut, Ethan called for the paramedic and his deputies while Maddie tried to visualize what she'd seen. There had been no signs of any injuries, but she'd seen blood outside, which meant they had to be behind him. Unless Buddy was killed in another manner and the blood outside wasn't his.

"Maddie?"

The insistent tone and Ethan's long-suffering expression made her think that it was probably not the first time he'd called her name.

"It's time for you to leave. I need to start investigating and to look for potential witnesses."

"I'm a witness," she protested.

"You've told me everything you know, right?"

Reluctantly, she nodded.

"Plus, I know where to find you."

She sighed. He was in sheriff mode and she would have to wait to get any information from him until he was good and ready.

"And Maddie? Please don't mention this to Laura."

"But—"

"Please."

"Okay." She was expected to go back to the bakery and pretend that all was well. Though she had tried hard not to think of it, Buddy's face flashed once more in her mind and she let out a shaky breath. Maybe she could fake not being upset in front of Luke and Laura, but Gran was an entirely different ball game.

Chapter Eight

"Where's the meat?"

Naturally, Laura was the first person Maddie saw when she arrived back at the bakery. Though she'd thought about Buddy the whole walk home, she wasn't completely prepared for how to keep his death to herself as Ethan had requested. "It isn't quite ready," she responded lamely, which wasn't a lie.

"That's not like Thomas. He's usually so organized." Laura frowned. "Are you okay? You look troubled."

"I'm fine. Lots to think about." Maddie deliberately distracted her, while feeling incredibly guilty about not sharing the news about Buddy.

Laura smiled. "Of course there is. Never mind about the meat. We have enough in the freezer for the pies, and if I can take the pressure off the wedding plans in any way, just let me know."

"Thanks, Laura. Say, what time did you get home Friday night?" Maddie asked casually.

Before her red-faced friend could answer, Gran came

through from the store wearing the widest grin. "It was close to midnight before Buddy brought her home."

When Maddie bought the store and decided to live above it, Laura was struggling to make ends meet and had moved into Gran's cottage. They were great company for each other and Laura was now like family.

Laura's cheeks burned. "Gran!"

Gran shrugged sheepishly. "Sorry, was it a secret?"

"No, of course not, but you don't have to tell the world about it," Laura protested. "Besides, we were outside talking for ages."

"I know."

Laura gasped and her red cheeks practically glowed. "You were listening?"

"Couldn't help hearing some of it, if I'm honest. He made you laugh. A lot."

"It sounds like a nice time was had by all," Maddie added casually. "What did the two of you have to talk about for so long?"

"All sorts of things," Laura hedged.

It was clear that Laura had enjoyed her date. Maddie couldn't help pressing even though she felt disloyal and worried how Laura would take the news. "Like?"

"Music, the bakery, parents, the usual stuff you talk about when you meet someone new."

"What did he tell you about himself?"

A dreamy look came into Laura's eyes. "He fell in love with music when he was very young and learned guitar early on. He's been performing since he was ten."

Maddie nodded. "He said he lived in Destiny. Where did he come from originally?"

"He's traveled a lot, and I think he said he came from

somewhere near Nashville." Laura suddenly frowned. "Why are you asking so many questions?"

Unable to lie to her face, Maddie washed her hands and mumbled, "Just curious."

She should have known that her grandmother would sense something was wrong. When Laura took a plate of cupcakes out to the counter, Gran appeared at her elbow. Knowing what was coming, Maddie almost wished she hadn't taken the opportunity to question Laura about Buddy.

"What's going on?" Gran hissed.

Maddie reached for a recipe. "I thought I'd get started on another trial of the honey cake."

Gran's hands slipped to her hips. "Don't play the innocent with me. That recipe is upside down. You've been up to something, haven't you?"

"I haven't. I went to the butcher's and then came home."

"Hmmm. We both know it doesn't take two hours to pick up meat from the end of the block," Gran said logically.

"Well, I did see Ethan." It was Maddie's turn to blush, but not for the reason Gran assumed.

"Now that makes sense. Did you two get in a fight?"

"Of course not."

"But he's annoyed with you?" Gran pressed.

On shaky ground, Maddie shrugged. "Maybe a little."

"My dear girl, you have to let him think he has some say in the wedding, even if most of the time he couldn't care less about the details."

"You're right. I'll try to remember that next time we discuss it."

"It will all work out fine." Gran patted her shoulder but didn't move away. "Even if we need to pivot a little."

That sounded suspicious. "Did you have something to tell me?"

Gran sighed. "I do, but I wasn't sure how."

"Just say it."

"Your mom can't make it to the wedding."

All thoughts of Buddy flew out the window as disappointment slapped her in the chest. "Oh."

Gran wrapped her in a hug. "I'm so sorry. I know how much it means to you to have her here now that the two of you have made amends."

Maddie swallowed the lump in her throat. "It is a shame and I am disappointed, but you were always going to give me away."

It was no secret that she and her mother had not gotten on for most of Maddie's life. In fact, she had been brought up by Gran and Grandad instead of her parents. After her father left, Ava Flynn opted for a more transient lifestyle. It was her mom's cavalier attitude to leaving and barely showing up through the years that had hurt the younger Maddie. Thankfully, they'd found a way to forgive the past and accept that they were very different people.

Gran smiled. "Whew! I'm glad you're taking it so well, and you know I'm honored to do that. Ava was terribly upset about letting you down and didn't want to tell you over the phone. Since she bought the fudge store, business is booming, and they're also having some issues with the foundations on the castle. The timing couldn't be worse for that."

"The castle was in a terrible state of disrepair when we visited last year," Maddie conceded. "We saw first-hand how it's an ongoing job to keep it looking its best. I'm sure it is hard to get away with the latest worry, but I'm glad the business is doing so well."

"You're such a wonderful daughter." Gran sniffed. "I know your mom will appreciate your understanding, and she promised to come over from England as soon as she can manage it."

"That will be nice. Plus, you won't have house guests for the week around the wedding, which will be good for you—less stress."

"I'm barely seventy and I didn't mind at all," Gran protested. "Speaking of houses, have you decided where you'll live yet?"

"Please don't ask. We're going around in circles over it. Being able to get out of bed, shower, and be at work in fifteen minutes is too hard to contemplate giving up right now."

"I agree. Have you thought of renting Ethan's place out?"

"Not really. I guess it makes sense. Only I'm not sure he's given up trying to persuade me to move in there just yet."

They laughed, but Maddie sobered quickly when, after a brief rap, Ethan came through the back door and removed his hat.

"Morning."

"This is a nice surprise." Gran walked toward the doorway into the bakery. "I'll leave you two to talk."

"Actually, it's Laura I need to speak to."

Gran turned back to him and raised an eyebrow. "Laura?"

The redhead was returning with a tray of dirty dishes and side-stepped Gran. "I'm here. Do you need me for something?"

"Could we go somewhere private?" Ethan asked.

"You can use my apartment if you like," Maddie suggested, taking note of the color leaving her friend's face and unable to do a thing about it.

"Thanks. After you, Laura." Ethan waved the anxious woman forward.

Gran waited until they were upstairs and Ethan had closed the door to the apartment. "What's that all about?"

Maddie threw ingredients for the honey cake into the mixer and switched it on, hoping the noise would deter her.

"I knew it! You're hiding something. Is it to do with that entertainer?" Gran yelled.

She quickly flicked the Off switch, worried that their customers would hear. She assumed this was Gran's plan. Maddie faced her. "Why would you presume that?"

"I saw your face when you were asking all those questions about Buddy. Admittedly, you did a good job of deflecting your long absence onto the wedding. Now I see it was all a ruse so you wouldn't have to explain what happened while you were gone." Gran nodded, a touch of pride mixing with her annoyance. "Very clever."

While it was one thing to have talents for deduction and seeing the big picture in an investigation, just as her secret agent grandfather had taught her, the ability to hide things from Gran was rarely on Maddie's list of achievements.

She wavered. "Can you wait a little while longer? I promised Ethan I wouldn't talk about it, and since we're about to be married, I'd like to keep at least one promise."

Gran sniffed. "Well played, dear. After being married to your grandfather for so long and raising your mother, both with far too many secrets and absences, I had to learn patience. Which doesn't mean I like it."

If the shoe were on the other foot, Maddie would feel

the same way. She let out a long breath. "Thanks for under-standing. I better get this cake in the oven."

"Then I may as well go help Luke out the front. Good-ness knows how long Ethan will keep Laura."

They both glanced up the stairs.

"Hopefully not too long," Maddie muttered. In her experience, the longer an interview with the police, the more likely the person interviewed would find themselves in hot water.

Chapter Nine

Ethan tucked his notebook in his pocket as he came down the steps and their eyes met.

Maddie crossed the room and looked up behind him. "How is she?"

He shook his head, then nodded for her to follow him to the back door. "Not good," he said quietly. "She's in shock and kept repeating that he was so nice that she couldn't imagine anyone hurting him, and that he was so full of life that she also couldn't contemplate he'd consider suicide."

She gasped. Suicide hadn't entered Maddie's mind. "Poor thing. Can I go see her?"

"Of course."

She hesitated. "Any updates on Buddy."

"Not that I can share."

"But it was murder, right?"

He sighed. "Obviously you saw his condition, so I'm going to say yes, but for now, you should keep this as quiet as you can. I still need the coroner's report to corroborate that."

She felt dreadful about mentioning it, but couldn't help

herself. "You don't think it has anything to do with the wedding?"

"Not at all. You'd only just met him and I never have, so how would anyone connect us?"

His insistence helped and she nodded. "It does put a dampener on it, though."

Ethan pulled her to him. "Listen to me, fiancée. We are not postponing this wedding. I've waited too long as it is to marry you. Nothing is going to stop me putting a ring on that finger in two weeks, and if that sounds harsh in light of Buddy's demise, then so be it."

Taken off guard, Maddie forgot everything else as her knees went a little weak when he kissed her firmly. When they finally broke off, she smirked. "Actually, I quite like the forcefulness, Sheriff."

"Oh." He blushed, then looked pleased with himself. "I see. I shall have to bear that in mind for future reference. Now, go see your friend so I can clear my head. I'll be back to talk to Gran about the timing soon."

She watched him leave and took a minute to come back to the problem at hand. Rekindling the love she'd had as a teenager for Ethan had come as a surprise and now she couldn't imagine life without him. Having come full circle, she wanted her dear friends to find the same sort of happiness, which was why she had encouraged Laura on her date.

Though Angel was a terrible flirt, she'd previously been married and it hadn't been a good one, so understandably she was wary. Driven and focused on her career, Suzy didn't seem to be bothered about the lack of dates. Laura was so shy talking to men, it was painful for her—and for everyone else to witness. When Buddy appeared and Laura had hit it off so well with him, Maddie had high hopes, despite Rob's interest.

Shaking her head at where her thoughts had gone, she climbed the stairs and found her friend curled into a ball on the sofa, sobbing into her hands. Maddie sat beside her. Not usually one for shows of affection, Laura allowed herself to be pulled into Maddie's arms.

"You already knew he was d-d-dead, didn't you?" Laura sniffled against her neck.

"Yes. I found his body. There was nothing anyone could do."

"Ethan said he died hours ago. In the middle of Saturday night or Sunday morning. Sometime after he left me," she wailed.

"I imagine so."

"I saw him drive off in his car. Why didn't he go straight home? I'm sure he wasn't sick."

Maddie squeezed Laura's slim shoulders. "We won't know that until Ethan and his deputies make inquiries."

"I just can't believe it. We got on so well. He's the first man who treated me like I was interesting."

Maddie leaned back a little. "What about Rob?"

"He's okay, but he's hot and cold. I don't understand him. Buddy was easy to talk to. And he was so talented. He should have been a big star."

Maddie frowned. "I wonder why he wasn't."

"I don't care about that. What matters is finding out why he was killed."

Maddie didn't like the gleam in her friend's eyes. "Did Ethan say he was killed?"

Laura raised an eyebrow. "He was found in a chiller. I don't supposed he'd mistakenly popped in there for a nap."

The sarcasm was so unlike Laura that Maddie blinked hard. "Well, no. I just don't see what his connection was with the butcher's shop when Thomas said he didn't know him."

"Do you think he was lying?'

"Why would Thomas lie about it?"

"If he killed him, he'd definitely lie about it. Wouldn't he?"

Maddie took a limp hand. "Think about it, Laura. Buddy was found in the chiller. If Thomas wanted him dead, he would have disposed of the body. He's up super early, like me. He could have used his truck and disposed of the body by the time I got there."

"Unless he was waiting until you left."

"Customers could have arrived at any minute. Besides, the shop was broken into, which means that someone wanted to dispose of Buddy." Maddie bit her lip. Ethan had probably not wanted her to reveal that, but it was too late to take it back. "It simply doesn't make sense for it to be Thomas."

"Then who did it?" Laura wailed again.

"I don't know, but Ethan will find out."

Laura stared at Maddie for a few heart beats until her eyes narrowed. "If he doesn't, then you have to. I'll help and so will the Girlz."

Maddie grimaced. Her mild-mannered friend had turned into a red-headed fury, and she wasn't sure how to calm the anger that burned so brightly. "Let's give Ethan a bit of time. It's only been a few hours since Buddy was found and there is so much evidence to go through."

Laura sat back against the arm of the sofa. "My head hurts."

Maddie put a hand on her shoulder and squeezed. "I can only imagine how you feel. This has been such a lot to take in and it's hard not knowing why. Why don't you take the rest of the day off and go home?"

"I can't. There's work to do and I don't want to let you down."

"You're not letting anyone down. Everyone gets sick days and this definitely qualifies as major stress."

Laura parted her lips, then let them slowly close as the fight drained out of her. "If you're sure you don't mind."

"Not only do I not mind, but I also insist." Maddie moved to the door. "Come on. I'll walk you home."

Laura stood and shook her head. "I'll be fine. The walk will be good for me and I'd like to be alone for a bit."

Watching her go, Maddie's heart ached for her friend. Hopefully she would get a little rest and therefore some respite from the questions that surely raced through her mind as they did her own.

Laura's plea for Maddie to help out with the case certainly didn't help matters.

Chapter Ten

Ethan didn't return until after lunch. Following a quick chat with Gran, he asked to speak to Luke. Maddie had made a point of avoiding talking about anything other than Laura having a terrible headache and needing to go home, so Luke was none the wiser about Buddy.

They sat at the kitchen table and Maddie busied herself with yet another honey cake, guilt pressing between her shoulders. Since they were only several feet away from her, she heard every word.

Ethan had pulled out his notebook and opened it. "I hear you're a big fan of Buddy Preston?"

Luke snorted. "So that's what all this is about."

The sheriff raised an eyebrow. "All what?"

"You lot sneaking around and whispering."

"You noticed," Ethan said casually.

So casually Maddie could tell he was testing Luke and she didn't care for it.

The young man shrugged. "I'd have to be deaf and stupid not to see that something's going on."

"Why didn't you mention your suspicions?"

"I figured if you wanted me to know, you'd tell me in good time. And if it's to do with the wedding, then that's hardly my business." He frowned. "I guess it's not though, since you have that notebook out. We all know that means trouble."

"Fair enough," Ethan conceded. "Where were you on the weekend—starting with Friday night?"

"Friday night I went to the pub for a couple of hours. I went straight home after work on Saturday and spent the evening playing video games with a friend." He blushed. "Sunday, I had a picnic with a different friend."

Maddie measured ingredients for the third time, noting that Ethan didn't ask about those friends. Likely it was the same one—a certain apprentice hairdresser. In the year she'd known Luke, he'd matured so much. She was incredibly proud of her protégé, who had once been accused of a crime himself, and it troubled her to know he had more heartache coming.

"Please tell me as much as you can about Buddy."

Luke scratched his head for a minute. "What did he do? I'm thinking this is not about his ability to perform at the wedding."

"I'm afraid not." Ethan leaned forward. "Buddy Preston was found dead earlier today."

Luke reared back. "No way! I thought you were going to talk about him doing drugs when he was younger. Is that what killed him?"

Ethan raised an eyebrow and made a note. "The postmortem isn't done yet. Did you know him personally?"

Giving up all pretense of baking, Maddie noted that Ethan didn't add that any information from the postmortem wouldn't be available for some while.

"We met a few times." Luke gave a sad smile. "To be honest, I was a bit of a groupie around him and often got to chat after the shows when he had time and could be bothered to hang around bars attached to the smaller venues he performed in."

"What did you talk about?" Ethan pressed.

"Mostly music. Sometimes, it was the state of the world." Luke's mouth quivered a little. "Occasionally, we compared notes on growing up with a tough father who thought you weren't good enough." He shrugged. "Or weren't good at what they thought more worthy than what you were passionate about."

Ethan didn't ask for clarification. Luke's history was no secret. His father, who was trying harder these days, had certainly treated Luke poorly in the past.

"Do you know if Buddy was in contact with his family?"

"I don't think so. He'd gotten himself straight and was looking to settle down. At least that's what he told me." Luke glanced down at his shoes. "He said he wished he'd been smarter about things when he was my age."

"So he wasn't doing drugs anymore?"

"Not for a while. He liked a drink but drew the line at two as he was worried about swapping one addiction for another."

"Very sensible," Gran said as she cruised by with a tray of dirty cups.

Ethan raised an eyebrow at her but carried on with the interview. "Do you know of anyone who had an issue with Buddy? Anyone who harassed him at his shows or in those bars?"

Luke thought for a moment then shook his head. "I can't think of any incidents off hand. He was pretty likable."

"Buddy must have been almost double your age. Why do you think he spent so much time with you?"

The question not only surprised Luke, but Maddie and Gran who frowned at each other.

"Maybe I've misled you," Luke backtracked. "At first we didn't spend any time together. Sure, we were in the same room, but people were chatting and not really with me. I was just a hanger-on hoping to get a minute to talk with Buddy."

Ethan looked up from his notebook. "And obviously at some stage that did happen."

"Yeah. I couldn't believe it. One night at the bar, when the guy he was sat next to went to the restroom, I took the opportunity to introduce myself and offered to buy him a drink. He accepted an OJ and asked me if I was a fan. When I said yes, he told me to take a seat. We got chatting and time flew by. He said he really enjoyed talking to me and the next time he performed, when Buddy saw me, he motioned me to follow him backstage."

"What did he want with you back there?" Ethan's casual question held a wealth of innuendo.

Luke's eyes widened. "Nothing. He picked up his jacket and then we went to the local bar and talked some more. He seemed to genuinely like my company." Luke shrugged again. "I guess when I let it slip about my dad, we found out we had a painful time in common and that meant something."

The bell for the bakery front door sounded and when Gran stayed where she was, Maddie went through to the counter. As annoying as it was not to hear more, there was no doubt in her mind that Gran would relate what she heard once Ethan left.

Mavis Anderson and Nora Beattie took their usual table in the corner and waited expectantly.

"Good day, ladies. What can I get you?"

"We've been wondering about the seating arrangements for the wedding," Mavis said with deceptive innocence.

Usually tolerant of the busy bodies, Maddie wasn't in the mood today. "And why would you be wondering about that?"

Nora sniffed at her tone. "Well, we don't want to be put near the restrooms or the kitchen."

"Since I haven't worked on them yet, I can't promise anything."

"You do know those spaces are for the people you like least."

It was all Maddie could do not to roll her eyes. "Thanks for pointing it out, Nora. I shall bear it in mind when I do get around to it. Now, is it the usual coffees? What about the muffin of the day?"

Nora's eyes lit up. "Are we paying?"

"Nora!" Mavis squealed.

"Quit yelling at me." The grumpy woman pursed her lips. "It's a sad day when a person can't ask a fair question."

"Maddie has a business to run and a wedding to pay for, which we're invited to. Helping her have a special day shouldn't come with any expectations."

These two arguing was nothing new, and though Nora was irritating at times, when she hung her head, Maddie got a sense that something was troubling the woman. "Listen, I appreciate everything you're doing for me and Ethan. How about a compromise? You both get free coffees until the wedding but pay for any food?"

"That sounds very reasonable even if it isn't necessary." Mavis nudged her friend.

Nora nodded. "What about Irene? She's helping too."

Maddie smiled, reminded again that Nora wasn't all prickles. "Of course. The three of you are a package."

"Just like you and the Girlz." Mavis grinned. "Only a slightly older version."

Nora snorted, then they all laughed, until Maddie remembered poor Buddy Preston.

"Let me get these coffees for you." She hurried to the doorway to peek inside the kitchen. Ethan had gone and Luke loaded the dishwasher while Gran put the honey cake into the oven.

She'd make the coffees, then see if Luke would prefer to go home as well. It sounded as if he had gotten close to Buddy and was bound to be as upset as Laura. Probably more so, since he had known him a lot longer.

Chapter Eleven

After Maddie delivered the order to Mavis and Nora, she hurried out to the kitchen where Gran was busy cleaning up the counters.

"I hope you don't mind, but I sent Luke home. He was grateful, and I don't think he could have handled dealing with customers today."

"Great minds and all," Maddie mused. "I was coming to suggest that very thing. From the way he spoke about Buddy, it was natural he'd be upset by the musician's death. Did he say anything more about it?"

"Not to me, but he did say to Ethan that he was shocked and angry if it was murder. Ethan didn't buy into the argument, which was wise."

Maddie nodded. "He won't want Luke looking for his own answers, though it will be hard not knowing why this happened to Buddy."

"It's an awful thing for anyone to accept, and Luke is so caring." Gran dabbed the corners of her eyes. "What saddens me the most is that he doesn't have a lot of friends, thanks to his father and brother knocking his self-esteem for so many years. It sounded like he and Buddy had found a common bond despite the age gap, and now Luke's lost a friend."

Maddie put her arm around Gran's shoulders. "It is sad. I just hope he doesn't bottle it all up inside and not talk to anyone about it. Maybe I should encourage Beth to phone him if she hasn't heard from Luke by tomorrow."

"That's an excellent idea. Though it might pay to go through Angel. Beth likes and respects her and is wary of everyone else poking into her business."

Angel's apprentice was close to Luke's age and they got on well, but Beth had an issue with authority. Before working in the salon, she'd had a huge problem with people in general. "You're right. She'll likely run a mile if I approach her."

"I don't know about that, but it wouldn't help Luke if she did. Her aloofness can still be an issue, but she's making headway in her studies and with customers. I'm sure she'd want to help Luke if she could. Besides, Big Red loves Beth, so she has to have a good heart."

Hearing his voice, Big Red arched his back just outside the back door, did a three-sixty and curled back into a ginger ball. He might be bossy at times, but he had the ability to make them smile when times were difficult.

"He does have a good sense of character," Maddie mused. "I'll ask Angel tonight if she could broach the subject."

Gran set the dishwasher into motion. "Are the Girlz coming over tonight to go over the seating plan for the wedding?"

A finger to her lips, Maddie shot a look at the doorway. "Yes, but please don't say anything about that to Mavis or

Nora. They've told me categorically where they don't want to sit."

"Is that right?" Gran huffed. "If you have any issues with those two, you leave it to me to sort out."

Maddie laughed. "You might be sorry you said that."

"Not at all. It's your wedding and you get to decide who sits where. I won't have them putting pressure on you about anything. They're lucky to be invited."

"Gran, they're your good friends. It was impossible to leave them off the list, and I do want everyone to enjoy themselves."

"If they don't, it won't be through any fault of yours, and we can just as easily uninvite them if they misbehave." Gran's face softened. "I do hope Laura will join you tonight. Sitting at home dwelling on Buddy won't do her much good."

Maddie had also been worrying about her friend. "She only found out this morning. We need to give her a little time to work through this, so don't push her into coming if she's not up to it."

"I wouldn't dream of it."

The innocent look didn't fool Maddie. They both knew her grandmother had a will of iron when it came to mothering her Girlz and making sure they didn't suffer if she could find a way to prevent it.

It was Gran's passion for baking that had led to Maddie learning the skills and eventually owning her own bakery. She would be forever grateful to be living her childhood dream thanks to Gran's determination to bring her home from Manhattan. The means had been sneaky, but it had all worked out, with the bonus of the bakery being near Gran's cottage at the end of the lane.

Living so close and working part-time also meant that

Gran could cover any eventuality at the bakery—like today. Gran stayed for the rest of the afternoon and as soon as they closed, she hurried home to check on Laura.

Chapter Twelve

Maddie took the casserole she'd prepared earlier upstairs and made another trip for a plate of garlic bread and a honey cake for after dinner. Suzy and Angel arrived together right after work and Gran phoned with Laura's apology.

"This smells amazing and I'm starving!" Angel plated up for all of them and took a hunk of the bread.

"What's wrong with Laura?" Suzy demanded around a mouthful of bread.

Though she'd expected the question, it was still so surreal that Maddie took a deep breath before explaining about Buddy.

"Wait!" Angel gasped. "The guy from Friday night? Laura's date?"

"That's right. After I called Ethan about the blood and hat outside Thomas's place, we found him dead in the chiller."

Suzy shuddered. "That couldn't be an accident, could it?"

"Ethan doesn't want any conjecture just yet," Maddie told them lamely.

Angel waved her spoon at Maddie. "We all know what that means. Precisely nothing."

Suzy nodded. "There's no way you'll stay out of the case."

"What do you mean?"

"Oh, please! You're like a dog with a bone every time there's a mystery to solve. This fits the bill and Laura's involved."

"Suzy's right, but you have to ignore the urge," Angel pleaded. "Especially with the wedding so close."

Suzy rolled her eyes. "You're delusional if you think that will stop our amateur sleuth."

Maddie bristled, but only for a second. To be fair, she had involved her friends in a few cases already since she came home. "Look, I admit I'm intrigued as well as being upset about his death, but I'm not risking the wedding for a near stranger."

"Nice words, Agatha," Suzy scoffed, "but I ain't buying them."

"Oh no!" Angel's spoon clattered to the table. "If Buddy's dead, what are you going to do for music?"

Maddie grimaced. "I hadn't thought of that and it seems a bit callous to do so this soon."

"Nonsense." Angel brushed the idea away. "It's absolutely awful, but you can't change the fact that he's dead, so we need to think of another musician soon—or we'll have to do Karaoke."

"Oh, no we won't." Maddie tapped her thigh at the threat of these two commandeering a microphone. "There has to be a better solution. I only got Buddy because Luke knew him and I couldn't possibly ask him for another recommendation."

"I don't see why not." Suzy shrugged. "I mean, if he's a music buff, he'll know more musicians or at least have some ideas where to look for someone suitable."

Angel shook her head sadly. "Oh, Suzy. Sometimes I worry about the children in your care."

The petite principal stiffened. "What do you mean by that?"

"Where is your sympathy? Do you dismiss your pupil's feelings so easily? Or do you keep this side of you hidden from them?"

"I wasn't dismissing Luke's feelings, and my children and their parents love me." Suzy huffed.

Knowing they both cared about Luke and Laura, and were only trying to keep her mind off the murder, Maddie smiled. "Principals have to be a little forceful at times, but Suzy's right about the way her parents and children adore her."

"Lucky them," Angel said dryly. "Now, who could we get? Hey, I have an idea. What about Noah Jackson?"

"A deejay? What a great idea!" Maddie sighed deeply. "Why didn't we think of him before?"

Angel patted her arm. "Don't go thinking that if we had, Buddy would be alive."

"I didn't.... Okay, it did cross my mind."

"Of course it would, but that's plain ludicrous," Suzy said pointedly. "How could hiring Buddy to be your wedding singer encourage someone to kill him?"

"Unless they don't like weddings," Angel suggested. "Or Maddie."

Maddie shook her head. "That's not funny. "

"I know, but I don't want you to be sad when we're

talking about your wedding. Hurry up and finish your meal so we can get started on the seating arrangement."

Suzy's eyes bugged at Angel's plate. "You've finished already?"

Angel put a manicured hand to her mouth and gave a soft burp. "I told you I was hungry."

An easel stood near the kitchen counter with a cork board resting on the tray. Tacked onto this was a sketch of the community center. The bridal table ran lengthways down the room and had seating for ten.

On one edge of the table, two pins in the middle held the names Ethan and Maddie. On Maddie's immediate right was Angel's name, followed by Suzy, Camille, and then Laura. On Ethan's left was his sister, Layla, Deputy Robert Jacobs, Detective Steve Jones, and Bernie Davis.

The guest list was as small as they could make it and they had to seat the sixty guests ten to a table to fit the room. Gran had asked for the table immediately in front of the bridal table where she could help watch over Layla's twin boys who were a handful. Without Ethan, if anyone else could keep them in line it would be Gran.

"I think the loudest people should sit the furthest away." Angel pinned the cards for Nora and Mavis into the table by the kitchen."

Maddie gasped. "Do you want to start a riot? I told you what they said."

"Well, you can't have everyone at the front tables, can you, sugar? Sometimes you have to be tough to get a job done. Goodness knows how I'd get their haircuts done if I didn't stand firm by ignoring their suggestions—and digs at my ability."

Knowing exactly what Angel meant about the many questions and in Nora's case, complaints, that the two friends subjected everyone to, Maddie sighed. "We should have eloped."

"And I never would have spoken to you again," Angel told her matter-of-factly.

"Sure you would have." Maddie nudged her. "Eventually. Anyway, you're being a bit hypocritical since you did elope."

Angel sniffed. "That was completely different. I was too young to see sense, had no money, and look how that turned out."

"Okay, okay." Maddie decided she shouldn't have brought it up. Angel's marriage was a disaster, which they didn't need any reminders of. "Who can I sit them with?"

"Put them with my parents," Suzy suggested. "Dad will have a few beers and not pay them any mind and Mom will be flitting around the room as usual."

"Thank you!" Maddie beamed.

With the hardest to please guests sorted, the rest of the seating went well. They had just put in the last card when they heard someone come in downstairs. Big Red flew down the steps and a minute later, returned with Gran.

She was pale and her hands shook as she held them out beseechingly to Maddie. "You must do something."

Hurrying to put her arms around the shaking body, Maddie hugged her. She had rarely seen her grandmother so upset and it frightened her. "What's happened?"

"I can't believe it." Gran's voice still shook, but she pulled herself together. "Ethan came to the cottage and took Laura."

Also upset, because she loved Gran almost as much as Maddie, Angel was now on Gran's other side. "Took her where?"

"To the station. He arrested her for Buddy Preston's murder."

"What?" Suzy snorted. "He can't have. I mean, why would he?"

"I was there." Gran fumed. "They have evidence that she was the last person to see him alive."

Maddie shook her head at the ridiculousness of the situation. "That doesn't make her guilty of murder."

"According to Ethan, there is other evidence."

"I don't understand, Gran. What could possibly link Laura to this apart from one date?"

Gran took Maddie's hand and squeezed. "He wouldn't tell me any more—but he'll tell you."

Maddie shook her head again. "I don't think that he'll be able to tell me much."

"You have to try."

"Of course I will," Maddie assured her. "I just don't want you to pin everything on it. Remember, Ethan has a job to do, and he knows Laura. He wouldn't have arrested her if he could have avoided it. I have no doubt that he'll already be looking for something to prove her innocence."

Suzy paced the room. "What if Buddy attacked Laura and she had to fight him off?"

Maddie blinked several times as she tried to picture it. "He didn't seem the type and even if he was, that would mean that Laura possibly did kill him. I can't get my head around that."

"Self-defense is a good enough reason," Angel added thoughtfully. "I had heard of his music and although I didn't know the man, it is angsty. You obviously formed a favorable opinion, but you didn't spend much time with him, did you?"

"No," Maddie admitted. "He was a stranger before

Friday. Anyway, we can go back and forth about this, but Laura is our friend and I can't stay here wondering. I know it's late, but I'm going down to the station."

"Ethan told me you shouldn't." Gran's voice held little conviction. "That's why I didn't phone you. I wanted to ask you face-to-face. Please help Laura, but don't do anything silly and ruin your relationship with Ethan."

Maddie kissed her cheek. "He'll know that I won't listen, and we love each other too much for this to affect us. If Laura needs a lawyer, I want to get onto it right away. I doubt she'll have the funds to organize it herself."

"I'll chip in for one," Suzy offered immediately.

Angel nodded. "Me too."

"I have money you should use first," Gran insisted.

"Thank you all. I know Laura will be grateful, but let's find out what we need first. Suzy, can you see Gran home?"

Before Suzy could reply, Gran took a seat on the sofa. "I'd rather stay here with Big Red if that's okay? I want to hear as soon as you know what's happening, but the Girlz should go home. You all have work tomorrow."

The ginger cat rubbed himself against Gran's legs and jumped up beside her. Maddie knew they would take care of each other. "I don't know how long I'll be, but of course you can."

Angel took a seat beside Big Red. "We'll stay with her."

Suzy bustled into the kitchen. "I'll make some tea."

Maddie loved these women and gave them a watery smile as she grabbed her bag. "I'll be back as soon as I can."

Chapter Thirteen

Since the station was down Main Street, Maddie let herself out the front door and hurried along the shop fronts. The station sat opposite the library. Finding the door was locked, she pressed the buzzer with a shaky hand.

Deputy Robert Jacobs unlocked the door, but barred her entry. "I'm sorry, unless it's an emergency, I can't let you in."

"An emergency? I'd say it is, Rob! You've arrested Laura for something she couldn't have done."

His gaze was cooler than she had ever seen. "She wasn't arrested and there is a process for these things, which we are smack in the middle of. It takes time to interview a suspect and to get statements down and signed as you are well aware of."

Maddie's heart sank. The sweet man she thought she knew had left without a trace. "I do know all that, but it's Laura! You know her, too, Rob. She wouldn't hurt a fly."

He glared at her. "No one is above the law, and obviously we don't always know people as well as we'd like to think."

She couldn't help her eyes narrowing as her temper rose. "Is this about her having one meal with Buddy? Because it sure sounds like it."

Rob stiffened. "Whatever Laura was doing or not doing prior to the murder isn't relevant to what happened afterward. I'm a professional simply doing my job, which I would like to get back to. I'm sure the sheriff will speak to you when he can. Goodnight." Rob tried to close the door, but Maddie put her foot in the way.

"She needs a lawyer."

"One has been provided."

Maddie blinked. She hadn't expected that, which somehow made the situation seem much worse, making her heart pound in her ears. If Laura needed a lawyer, then they had to be reasonably convinced she was guilty of killing Buddy. "When can I see her?"

"Tomorrow during daylight hours—if the sheriff allows it."

He stared down at her foot and she shuffled back. The door closed and he walked away without so much as a "goodnight".

Maddie wanted to scream at the unfairness and ridiculousness of the situation. Not knowing what evidence they had against Laura made it difficult to understand why she was being held. And Rob could say what he liked; he wasn't unbiased. Fuming as she walked down the street toward the bakery, she went through the facts as she knew them.

Laura had only been in Maple Falls for a couple of years at the most, but she'd already proved that's she was good and kind. She worked hard and helped Gran with the farm in lieu of board. Shy and old-fashioned in many ways, accepting the "date" with Buddy had been a surprise, but there was no hint that she was capable of having a break-down of some kind and hurting anyone. No matter the reason.

Although, Suzy's suggestion about self-defense was a good one. Maddie had been in situations where she'd had to fight for her life and where a person could unwittingly do another harm. What could that scenario look like for someone like her friend? Laura was fit. You had to be to bake the hours they did as well as lift and carry heavy pans. None of that made her physically capable of fighting off a man.

With no blood stains on the path to Thomas's as there were at the back door, Buddy had likely been carried rather than dragged into the chiller. Though he wasn't a huge man, he was tall and would have weighed a significant amount. Laura was slight and only the same height as Maddie's 5'7". It would have been difficult even if he had been killed nearby for her to move him by herself. In fact, she doubted one person could have carried him.

Then there was the hat. Buddy wore a Stetson and with Laura dressed a little old-fashioned and always with her hair in a bun, the cap could not have belonged to either of them.

Maddie's feet slowed as she tried to recall if there was any insignia on the cap, and having crossed the street, she paused outside the butchery, which had likely been closed all day.

The Laura she knew wouldn't have a clue how to break in and of all the places to dispose of a body, why choose a butcher's?

None of this made sense. It was as if someone wanted to frame Laura, but she couldn't think of one reason. As far as she knew, no one in town had a problem with her. Of course, Laura had an issue with her parents, her mom in particular, but Laura hadn't seen them in months. It seemed a step too far if they wanted revenge for her not pursuing a career in politics. Actually, it would be the reverse, as they wouldn't want a child of theirs to have a criminal record. How would it look to their friends in high places?

Head pounding, Maddie turned away from the store. With a heavy heart, she made her way home and trudged upstairs, upset at having nothing positive to tell the women waiting for her.

Once she got to the landing, Angel hurried to her side and dragged Maddie to the sofa. "You look terrible. Did you see Laura?"

"How is she?" Gran demanded.

"Did you get her a lawyer?" Suzy asked.

Maddie put up a hand to stop more questions. "Rob wouldn't let me into the station. To be fair, Ethan probably told him there were to be no visitors, but you should have seen Rob's face. He was so angry."

"Angry about you being there?" Angel growled. "He's crazy if he thought you wouldn't at least try to see her and make sure she's okay."

"Actually, I'm convinced his anger was for Laura."

"What? She's the victim here," Suzy tutted. "After Buddy."

Maddie slumped back on the sofa. "I don't think he sees it all that way."

"Oh... he's upset about the date." Angel sighed. "Men can be so silly."

Suzy shrugged. "You can see his point a little. What a way to find out that your girlfriend is seeing someone else."

"No, I can't see his point." Angel growled. "He knows Laura and they're friends. You can't simply assume the worst about someone because they had a date. It's not like he and Laura are engaged or married."

Suzy's brow wrinkled. "I think in Rob's mind they were a couple, and I'm pretty sure Laura was hoping for that before Buddy came to town."

Gran nodded. "That is true. Let's not think too harshly of Rob until we hear all the facts."

"I would have said that was fair." Maddie shivered. "Except, you didn't see his face. His attitude scared me a little, and I admit that the idea of his seeking revenge by keeping us apart made me furious."

"I'm sure that wasn't his intention," Gran insisted. "He's naturally upset at the events and likely confused about his feelings. What about getting Laura a lawyer?"

Maddie shrugged, not exactly appeased by Gran's take on things. "According to Rob, she already has one."

"If Laura mentioned she didn't have and couldn't afford one, it will be a lawyer they've suggested," Gran said reasonably.

Maddie pursed her lips. "The fact that she needs one bothers me. I'm going down there first thing in the morning to see her and this time I'm not taking no for an answer."

Gran patted her hand. "Good for you. We need to know she is being represented properly and being treated fairly."

Maddie nodded bleakly. "I'm not convinced Rob doesn't have an issue and that he's being fair to Laura, but I know Ethan will make sure she's okay. I'm still hoping he'll drop by later or phone me."

After more tea, Maddie saw the Girlz and Gran out the

back door. Locking it after them, her hope died that she'd hear from Ethan. It was getting late and Big Red waited on the steps for her to go back up and get ready for bed.

"It's going to be a long night," she told him.

The ginger ball of fluff yawned and led the way. At least she'd have company.

Chapter Fourteen

Ethan didn't phone, nor did he drop by. He also didn't answer any of the texts Maddie sent him. Each one became more of a plea. Upset by his silence, Maddie was up before sunrise, barely sleeping a wink. Still, there was always a lot to do in the morning, and without Laura, her workload would be larger. Starting early would help, and once Luke arrived, they would manage until Gran came for her so-called reduced hours.

Supposed to be taking life easier, the septuagenarian loved being at the bakery. Once her animals were fed and she'd tidied the spotless cottage, Gran worked Tuesday to Fridays. There was no convincing her to go home early if she had a mind to stay.

An hour later, Luke came through the back door without his usual grin and swagger. After stowing his backpack in the corner of the office, he put on a clean apron.

"You don't have to work today if you're not up to it," Maddie called from over by the oven.

"I can't stay at home and think about Buddy. I'd rather keep busy."

Luke didn't meet her eyes and she suspected he'd been crying.

"Of course. Though you should feel free to take a break any time you need to."

"Thanks." He glanced around the bakery and then out toward the store. "Where's Laura? It's not like her to be late."

Maddie almost dropped the tray of bread she was carrying. Poor Luke already had one major upset to deal with and the news about Laura wouldn't help. Yet, she had to tell him before someone else did. Resting the tray carefully on the counter, she faced him. "Laura was picked up last night in relation to Buddy's murder."

"What?" He blinked several times as his face reflected all his feelings until it settled on rage. "That's the craziest thing I've ever heard!"

"I know. Gran came by last night and explained that Ethan turned up at the cottage with Rob. They took Laura into custody on suspicion of murder. I went down to the station as soon as I heard, but they wouldn't let me see her."

"They? You mean Ethan?" Luke growled.

She couldn't help the urge to defend her fiancé, but she was still annoyed at not being allowed to speak to Laura and at not hearing from Ethan. "Actually, Rob was the one who wouldn't let me in, but I suppose it would have been Ethan who gave the order," she admitted.

"How could either of them do that? She wouldn't be able to hide how scared she is and they must know that just seeing you would have made her feel a little better."

"Of course they do. I can only think that the evidence must be compelling. As soon as Gran gets here and we open, I'll get down to the station and make sure the lawyer they appointed is good enough."

"I guess at least her having a lawyer is something." Luke shook himself, then straightened his back. "I better get to work since we're short-staffed so you can leave as soon as possible."

Maddie was proud of his determination to deal with this and not fall apart. She'd witnessed that resolve once before—when his father had basically disowned him for not being "macho" enough to follow in his more physical footsteps.

She was also grateful that he was so supportive of both Laura and her. Gran might be a blood relation, but after the Girlz, Luke had come to feel like family too. With the pain of losing an idol, and now the worry over Laura, it was a lot for any twenty-year-old to deal with.

A scratching at the back door caught her attention and she opened it to scold Big Red, but all thought of that went out the window as he had merely been alerting her to a welcome sight. Gran was coming up the path arm in arm with Laura.

"Luke, come quickly!"

Even the clatter of dropped tins behind her didn't bother Maddie, and the next moment, Laura flew into her arms.

"Thank goodness you're out. Are you okay?"

Laura's head bobbed on Maddie's shoulder. "It was the worst night of my life and yet it was so surreal. When Ethan released me, I couldn't think straight, so he walked me home."

Pleased that Ethan had taken care of Laura, Maddie hugged her tightly. "I'm sure it was horrendous. I'm so sorry about Buddy."

"Last night, once they'd completed the interrogation, there was so much time to think about everything that happened. No one would talk to me and Rob couldn't look at me." Laura's voice hitched. "Then I thought about Buddy being gone and felt shallow about being so upset over one night in jail and Rob's attitude. I really liked Buddy. He seemed so nice and suddenly he's gone. I can't understand why anyone would want to kill him." Laura stepped back, her mouth quivering. "You do know it wasn't me?"

"Of course we know that," Maddie assured her rather forcefully. "The Girlz, Gran, and I wracked our brains to think of anyone who could be responsible, but it's difficult when we didn't know him."

Laura peered over her shoulder. "What about you, Luke? Any ideas?"

"No clue whatsoever," he said glumly. "There were the occasional people that heckled him, but not one person stands out in my mind. I already spoke with Ethan about it. They must have been clutching at straws to arrest you."

Laura sighed. "I guess they did have their reasons."

Everyone else gaped at the statement they hadn't seen coming.

Luke recovered first. "What reason could they possibly have?"

Cheeks pink, Laura clasped her hands in front of her. "Actually, there were a couple of things. Things that didn't occur to me right away, but could be construed as clues."

Gran frowned. "You talked about being released on our way here, but didn't mention any clues."

"What did they have on you," Maddie demanded.

Laura's knuckles turned white and she wouldn't meet their gaze. "I had Buddy's Stetson at home and my fingerprints were on his belt."

Mind boggling, Maddie took a deep breath. "Let's take this one step at a time. Why did you have Buddy's Stetson?'

"He let me try it on and then said I looked so good in it, I should keep it." Laura opened her arms. "Of course I said no, but he insisted and said he had plenty of them."

"Okay." Maddie decided that at least sounded reasonable. "And the belt? How did your fingerprints get on that?"

Gran leaned forward, but before she could speak, the bell over the store's door rang.

"I'll get it!" Luke backed out of the room; relief plastered on his face.

None of them might be ready to hear about whatever had gone on with Laura and Buddy, but Maddie nodded for her to go on.

As if sensing where their thoughts had gone, Laura lifted her chin. "I know it sounds bad, but it was completely innocent. When I admired the wolf head etched into the buckle, Buddy took it off so I could see it better. Nothing else happened. I handed it back when I was done and he put it back on the belt."

Though relieved by the confession, it hadn't made anything clearer. "It still doesn't seem enough to hold you for suspicion of murder."

Laura gave a jerky shrug. "That's what I thought until Ethan explained that added to my fingerprints inside his car and that I was the last person to see him, I was the most likely suspect."

"Hmmm. It still seems rather circumstantial to me." Maddie studied her friend who could be closed-mouthed about some things if they might make her look bad. It was understandable given her background, but this wasn't the time to hold things back. "Are you sure there wasn't anything else? And why did they release you?"

"I've racked my brain for something Buddy might have said, but we didn't talk about anything too serious." Laura grimaced. "Ethan said I was free to go, but to stay in town in case they needed to question me further."

"Let her be for now, Maddie," Gran intervened. "I'm sure the police are doing their best with the man power they have. It's been a long night and an emotional morning for all of us. We've been thinking of nothing else, so I'm sure Laura needs to forget about it for a while."

While she could see the hope in Laura's eyes, Maddie didn't want to forget about it. She knew that memories could fade or skew quickly after a terrible event, when people wanted nothing more than to forget it had happened. But Laura's determined look as she pulled on an apron told her they would get no further right now. "I see you're intending to work, but wouldn't you rather go home and rest?"

"I would have thought you of all people would understand." Laura sent a half-smile over Maddie's shoulder. "And I can see that Luke gets it."

Luke came further into the room and Maddie suspected that he had been biding his time until the awkward conversation was done.

He nodded. "I can't imagine anyone wanting to be alone with nothing to do and all these questions buzzing around their brain."

"If you're sure?" Maddie had to ask again.

"It was a horrible thing to happen, but sitting at home stressing over the why of it won't bring Buddy back." Laura locked eyes with her. "I have to trust Ethan to find the killer and this is where I said I'd be if he wants to talk to me some more."

Having been in a similar situation, Maddie did understand, but she was still frustrated by not knowing the why of Buddy's death. Plus, she couldn't forget how Laura was treated. If the police had evidence as Laura said, Maddie couldn't argue with that, but Rob's attitude had really upset her, and it had to have had an effect on Laura. Why wasn't her friend more bothered by it?

Plus, there was the wedding to consider. Was the murderer still in town? If so, was anyone else in their line of fire? And most importantly, did Buddy's death have anything to do with the wedding?

Maddie didn't see a connection, but experience had taught her that you could never tell in a murder investigation. Not until you had all the clues. Not until you found a way to piece them together. She couldn't do it without a little help, and Ethan seemed to be avoiding her which was incredibly frustrating.

Finding out why was her next step.

Chapter Fifteen

With a full contingency of staff, Maddie now had spare time if she needed it. And since Ethan wasn't getting back to her, she was determined to make use of the opportunity. Of course, the arrival of Nora, Mavis, and Irene was certainly what tipped her decision.

Deliberately avoiding the group and telling Gran she had some errands to run, Maddie tugged off her apron and hurried down Maple Lane to the back of Thomas's store. The hurry was due to the knowing look Gran sent her way as soon as she'd done giving her excuse. Very little got past Gran, which was sometimes annoying, yet it gave Maddie a warm glow that someone understood her so well. Her grandmother was in her corner no matter what.

Without giving it any further consideration, she went through the open gate and stood by the yellow tape that cordoned off the steps to the back door. Pushing as much as she dared against the tape, she noticed two things. The blood had been removed from the back door and all the windows on this side of the store, and the apartment upstairs, had the curtains closed.

Maddie hadn't given much thought to Thomas and how he'd be feeling right now. There had to be a lot of stress on him with the business closed until the police decided he could open again.

It was a fact that small town stores couldn't afford to lose customers. Though Thomas was bound to have insurance to replace the meat, which could have been potentially tainted by the killer and the police, people could be put off. She shivered. A body in a meat chiller wasn't appealing at all.

Since she couldn't get near the back door to knock, she headed around to the front. Face against the glass, she noted nothing moved inside. Maddie tapped on the door and repeated this a bit louder when no one came. Loathed to call out and draw attention from the shoppers or residents nearby, not to mention the police station across the street, she was about to leave when Thomas peeked around the corner of the small hall where the door to his stairs were located.

She beckoned to him. He seemed to hesitate before heading her way.

Glancing across the street at the station, he opened the door just a little. "I'm not supposed to talk to anyone."

This seemed extreme, but she nodded sympathetically. "I see. How long are you stuck inside for?"

"I'm not exactly stuck in here." He nodded to the station. "But they said I can't leave town. I don't know what to do. I mean, I can hardly sell the meat I have even when they do let me open, and I keep seeing that guy's face." He ran his hands through his hair. "This is a nightmare."

His anguish was obvious, and Maddie wished she could

help in some way. "What about staying at the resort for a couple of nights?"

Thomas snorted. "You might be able to afford a fancy wedding there, but that place isn't cheap. People like me don't have that kind of money laying around. And I have to watch every dollar when I have no idea how long I'll be closed for."

She didn't correct him on the wedding venue. "Surely you'll be allowed to open in a day or two?"

"Perhaps, but how many people will want to buy meat from where a dead man lay? This is probably going to ruin my business"

Maddie grimaced. "It may take a little time, but people will eventually forget."

"I hope you're right," he said despondently. "Anyway, what did you want?"

"It was such a terrible shock, and I was concerned about you. I just wanted to see how you are."

Thomas raised an eyebrow. "Yeah. I'm not buying that. While you're a nice woman and all, I think you want to find clues and solve the crime like you always do."

Her eyes widened. "Well...."

He cut her off with a snort. "You're so obvious, so let's not pussyfoot around."

"I'm obvious? Really?"

He nodded. "Yep and the sheriff told me to not let you in. Explicitly."

"Did he now? That's annoying."

Thomas suddenly croaked a laugh. "I figured you'd feel that way and I did wonder if your future husband stood any chance of corralling you." He glanced across the street again. "Better get inside if you're coming, but don't touch anything."

"If I had a dollar for every time I've been told that, I'd be rich," she muttered, a little miffed at the idea of being corralled. Following Thomas to the chiller, she was met with more tape. "That's a pain."

"Tell me about it. With the door being propped open for hours and the temperature all over the place, if I don't clean it out soon, it's gonna smell like rotten meat in here for weeks."

Maddie gasped. "I hadn't thought about that. Why won't they let you get rid of the meat if they've been through the chiller already and you're allowed to stay here?"

"The rest of the place has been cleared, but they're waiting on a specialist who they think might be able to find fingerprints on the meat, which could give them DNA or something."

Maddie blinked. "Of course. I hadn't considered it, but Grandad told me that you can get fingerprints off just about anything. I guess the killer had to move the meat to get Buddy in there."

He shuddered. "Your grandad sure knew a thing or two. It's a shame he's not here." He looked her up and down as if comparing the two Flynns and found her somewhat lacking. "I just wish they'd hurry up and get here."

He was naturally upset, annoyed, and fed up. Maddie had been in his position herself and it sucked big time not being able to run your store and not have a say in when you could open again. And her situation had only been a break-in. Sighing, she decided that since she couldn't get inside the chiller, then she should get back to the bakery. Unless... "Thomas, where were you when Buddy died?"

He shook a finger at her. "Hey, don't you go looking for a way to pin this on me like they did to Laura."

Thomas kept surprising her. "You know about that?"

He shrugged. "Everyone does by now. You know how it works around here."

She sighed again. "Gossip in Maple Falls moves faster than Big Red at meal time. Look, I don't believe you killed Buddy, but I am wondering why you weren't taken in for questioning and Laura was."

Thomas folded his beefy arms across his chest. "If it makes you feel any better, I did get taken in. I was interviewed at the same time as Laura."

Oddly, that pleased her. Not the interrogation part—she figured he wasn't being literal. It showed that Laura hadn't been the only suspect, which was a relief. It meant that the sheriff's department was spreading their net wider than she'd previously thought. With both suspects free, Ethan must be focused on finding the real killer and any leads she wasn't aware of, which could explain him ghosting her messages. Although, if he kept it up, she would be giving him her opinion on just how unacceptable it was.

She glanced around the store and through the door into the small hall. Were there leads here to be explored? "Can I have a look around upstairs?"

"What on earth for? Every inch of this place has been searched."

"I don't doubt that the sheriff's department was thorough, but things get missed even by the best."

He scratched his head before shrugging. "I guess it can't hurt as long as you don't tell anyone."

Maddie kept her mouth shut and followed him. She was more than capable of keeping things to herself—mostly. Unfortunately, Gran had a way of asking that made her spill secrets like a broken egg. Making a promise like that could result in her telling a big fat lie if Gran even slightly suspected she knew something. It wasn't something that she wanted to entertain.

The open-plan living was much like Maddie's apartment. Only, not quite so neat. Or clean. The furniture was well used, draped with clothing and bits and pieces of machinery. The kitchen sink overflowed with dishes.

"Excuse the mess. I haven't felt much like housework since I found the singer." His mouth turned down. "If I'm honest, I haven't felt much like doing anything."

"It will take some time, but you will get over this, Thomas," she promised.

"I don't know. The idea of someone wandering around my place makes me feel out of sorts. Like I've lost control of my life...." He looked away. "Don't mind me."

The fear in his voice was real, and if it wasn't for the folded arms, she might have hugged him. "You have a right to your feelings," she said gently. "Things like this touch us in ways no one can understand if they haven't experienced it. Now, I'm just going to have a quick look around, and if you come too, you can tell me if anything's been touched."

He followed her into the kitchen. "Why would they come up here if they were just looking for a place to, ah, dump the body?"

"I don't know about that." She peered out the window, which looked over Maple Lane. Across the road were Gran's fields and to the right stood the cottage. "But what if they were up here watching for Buddy?"

Standing close, he too peered out the window. "That would presume that the killer knew he was with Laura and was bringing her home." When he faced her, his eyes bugged. "Which in turn means he knows her and where she lives."

Maddie nodded. "Which probably means that the killer is either a local who wants to hurt Laura, or a jealous fan."

Chapter Sixteen

S till disappointed she couldn't get in the chiller, after a few words of encouragement, Maddie went back to the bakery. All of their conjecture was simply that and she hadn't found anything else at Thomas's place resembling a clue as to why the crime had been committed.

Nearly home, her phone rang. When she took it out of her pocket and saw who was calling, she stopped to answer it, unable to keep a little chilliness out of her voice. "Hello?"

"Where are you?"

She stalled at her garden gate, noting how tired he sounded, and deliberately stepped inside so she could tell him honestly, "At the bakery."

"Could you stop by the station?"

"What for?"

He sighed. "Please."

When she pictured him at his desk, stressed out by another murder, her heart melted. "All right. I'll be there soon." While she was annoyed that he hadn't returned any of her messages or calls, she understood he walked a fine line. He was a professional and she was his fiancée. A fiancée who liked to meddle. It wasn't easy for him, and she truly didn't want to make it harder.

Having a secret service grandfather who hid this from the whole town for many years, had set her on the path to wanting to solve mysteries. He'd made it clear that he didn't want Maddie following in his footsteps, but simply wanted her to be able to keep herself safe. Though her love of baking was the stronger desire, the result was she'd developed those skills and grown less afraid to use them. All this made Ethan worry more than he should have to. She stopped in at the bakery to get something and hurried out without seeing the others.

At the station, she was shown to his office by another deputy. This was a relief since she was still angry with Rob. Seeing the lines of tiredness around Ethan's eyes, she hurried around the desk to give him a hug. "How are you doing?"

He hugged her back and they both sighed.

"I'm fine," he murmured into her hair.

She leaned back to look him in the eyes. "No, you're not. Can I do anything?"

That made him snort. "How about you stay out of my case?'

The disbelief that this was a possibility made her smile. "I'm glad you saw sense and let Laura go."

Running his finger around his collar, he grimaced. "That wasn't my finest moment, but it was necessary."

There wasn't much Maddie could say about this when no matter how she hated it, she also knew it was true. "What was the lawyer like?"

Ethan shrugged. "He hardly spent any time here. We'd already decided to let her go."

"Hmm. Did you know that Rob was apparently not very nice to Laura while she was here?"

He shifted in his seat. "Yeah, I heard, and I had a word with him about that. It was awkward to say the least."

"I'm sure, but it wasn't at all professional on his part."

"No, it wasn't, but we're all human. Do you think Laura will forgive him?"

"I really don't know. She sounded so hurt when she spoke about Rob ignoring her."

He raised an eyebrow. "You've seen her already?"

"She's working today." Maddie gave a wry smile. "I told her to go home, but you know what she's like."

"Yeah, a workaholic, like you."

"I wouldn't throw stones, Sheriff. When did you sleep or eat last?"

Ethan suddenly noticed what she was carrying in her other hand. "To be honest, I haven't slept at all, and I'm starving."

Maddie placed the container on his desk and removed the lid to reveal two steak pies. "These are for you—I guess you could share with Rob."

The corners of his eyes crinkled. "That's very generous of you."

She shrugged. "As much as Laura did nothing wrong, I can see that Rob must have been upset about her being out with another man. Plus, it would have been a bigger shock to find out the way he did." Maddie paused for a moment to think. "Was it a coincidence that he called in to the bar that night?"

Ethan grimaced. "I believe someone mentioned Laura was there and he dropped by to see for himself. Poor guy was devastated."

Maddie blinked. "Devastated enough to do something about it?"

The pain in Ethan's voice came through. "As much as I want to tell you that's a ridiculous notion, the thought did cross my mind."

"And?"

"I checked on a couple of things and then dismissed it. While Rob potentially had a motive, he was working night shift."

With a huff, Maddie sat on the corner of his desk. "So you didn't even question him? I imagine with a chilled body it would be hard to pinpoint the time of death. After all, there were a lot of hours between Buddy leaving the cottage and us finding him."

"That's true, and rest assured that I did speak with Rob regarding his whereabouts. I'm satisfied that there is no way Rob would commit such a crime and dispose of the body like that. Besides, it would have taken some time to break in to Thomas's without anyone hearing and Rob's paperwork doesn't allow for that."

She nodded slowly, accepting that Ethan would know if the time frame was feasible or not. "I guess there are much easier ways to go about it. He could have driven Buddy out of town and dumped the body someplace it wouldn't be found for a long time."

Ethan nodded back automatically while he eyed the pie. "The problem is everyone is a suspect right now. We've begun interviewing people in the area and those at the bar that night. Logistically, it's a nightmare. I've had to call in Detective Jones."

"Oh, boy."

That got his attention. "Why do you say it like that?"

"No reason." When Ethan continued to stare at her, she

shrugged. "Look, I know he's good at his job, but he does rub people the wrong way."

He sighed. "Steve is a friend now and I thought you liked him too."

"With he and Angel having a little thing going, I've accepted him, but we're not exactly buddies like the two of you. He doesn't approve of my wanting to help," she finished lamely.

"Nobody in our profession does," he said a little too smugly before throwing up a hand. "We have to solve this crime soon, and if a few feathers get ruffled, so be it. I want to marry you and with this hanging over our heads, I can't see how that can happen."

She gasped. "You're actually contemplating postponing the wedding?"

"If necessary," he said firmly, then his voice softened. "I know it seems ridiculous that Buddy's death has anything to do with us, but without a clear motive, since you'd hired him and with Laura's involvement, I'd be scared to proceed."

Maddie blinked fast, determined not to cry. Ethan was right. They had to solve the murder very soon or all their plans would be wasted. "Then you better let me help."

"Seriously?" Ethan groaned. "That's what you got out of this conversation?"

"I want to marry you too. If you think I'm going to sit back and not do anything, then you don't know me at all."

"We've known each other most of our lives. I know you too well and that scares me too. I can't have you blundering around the case. Especially not once the detective arrives."

Taking exception to the blundering comment, she tapped her thigh. "When will that be?"

His eyes traced the movement, and he leaned back in his chair. "Very soon."

"Then you better fill me in on any clues so I can get out of your hair," she told him sweetly, forcing her fingers to still.

"That's not happening. Please try to stay out of this. It's my job and we need my salary if we're going to get our own place one day."

His clear bribe didn't miss the mark by too much. For him to be considering their future as a married couple always made her warm inside. "Fine. I'll do my best to stay out of the case and your hair." Pushing the container out of the way she leaned down and kissed him hard before pushing away. "I love you."

Running a finger along her cheek, his smile held a touch of regret. "You are trouble I can't deal with right now, but I love you too."

"Then put me out of your mind, Sheriff, but not every minute. You could message me occasionally to let me know you're okay. The worry isn't one-sided when you're engaged to a sheriff."

"Sorry about that." Ethan chuckled. "I guess you're marrying a wimp because I didn't know what to say if I did reply, and I knew you'd badger me for information."

Maddie could hardly be angry when he was being so honest. "You're anything but a wimp and I'm sorry too. I know it would be easier for you if I was different."

He grabbed her arms and pulled her down for a longer kiss. When they came up for air, he said, "I wouldn't change a single hair." Ethan tossed the thick braid brushing his cheek over her shoulder. "And I will do everything in my power to get this case solved in time for the wedding."

With a cheeky wink, and a lighter heart from having seen him, she slipped from his arms. "I'm counting on it, Sheriff."

Chapter Seventeen

Back at the bakery, Gran continued to roll out pastry while watching her. "You've been gone a while."

"Sorry I took so long. Ethan called me to the station," Maddie explained, omitting her visit to the butcher's.

Gran nodded to the store front. "Laura's at the mercy of Irene and her cronies."

Maddie snorted. "Woah! They're your friends."

"Friends I could happily gag right now." Gran tutted. "I've tried to do most of the serving, but they only have to spy Laura and they're throwing out twenty questions about the murder her way."

"It does seem to have gotten around exceptionally fast—even for Maple Falls."

Gran grimaced. "Now that you're back, perhaps you could go intervene. I have a splitting headache."

Concern immediately replaced any reluctance. "Do you want to go home?"

"No." Gran nodded at the store front again and growled, "I want *them* to go home."

Maddie chuckled as she washed her hands. "Wish me luck."

She found Laura backing away from the table where Gran's friends held court. "Good morning, ladies," she called with false cheerfulness. "Laura, Gran needs you."

The redhead rushed from the room as if her feet were on fire.

Mavis beamed at her. "Finally, someone who will know what's going on. Laura won't say a word."

Maddie pointedly held the tablet for taking orders at the ready. "I daresay I know about as much as you do."

"With a sheriff for a fiancé, I doubt that," Nora stated.

"He'd get into trouble if he told me everything about his cases."

"But maybe he did tell you something?" Mavis wheedled.

"Sorry, you're asking the wrong person."

"Apart from losing your wedding singer, will this murder affect the wedding?" Nora huffed.

"I hope not, and thanks for reminding me to check my list. I must catch up with Noah Jackson."

Irene's eyes widened. "Surely you're not hiring a deejay?"

"Don't look so horrified. He's a great deejay and we'll be able to have a variety of music this way." Maddie wasn't surprised by the shock on the well-dressed woman's face. Irene lived a great life at the retirement community and came from a wealthy family. Since Mavis was comfortable, and Nora struggled financially, they were more accepting of cost cutting.

"I imagine the list of available musicians would be small at such short notice," Mavis added reasonably.

"You're right about that," Maddie agreed. "And while

live music would have been nice, if Noah says yes, then that will be one less thing to stress about."

Mavis patted her arm. "I'm sure it will be a relief, and Gran said the seating is taken care of."

"That's right. The Girlz and I did it the other night and it will be a nice surprise for you on the day."

"You won't tell us that either?" Nora tutted. "Sometimes I wonder why we come in here."

"Here I was thinking it was for the food and the company," Maddie teased.

Nora studied her friends and sniffed. "Well, you are a good baker."

While the rest of the group looked outraged, Maddie laughed. "Thank you so much for the endorsement. Now, I'll get you more coffees so I can go find Noah."

"I saw him doing his bendy thing in the park earlier," Nora said with an edge of disdain.

Irene sighed. "That was hours ago, and it's called yoga."

"A weird name for a weird thing to do in public." Nora shook her head. "I swear if those pants were any tighter...."

"Okay, we get the picture. Yoga isn't for you. Maybe stay away from the park so early in the morning and you won't be subjected to seeing things you find upsetting," Maddie suggested.

Norah sniffed. "I always walk early in the morning and there they are."

Mind whirring, Maddie stepped closer. "Yes, you do. Did you happen to see anyone around town the morning Buddy was killed?"

"I guess you mean the singer? Unless we've had another murder," Nora said dryly. "What do you mean by anyone?"

"A stranger, or someone who isn't usually out that early."

Nora closed her eyes and tilted her head. "It was a nice morning, and the sun was just peeking over the horizon. Jed was walking Sissy down Main Street. That red setter of his was prancing around showing off. She licked my hand when I stopped to give her a pat."

This was an almost whimsical depiction from the snarky Nora and had Maddie and the other women gaping at her as she continued.

"I walked by the twisted group and up to Gran's cottage at the end of the Lane. When I passed the back of the shops, everything was quiet. Though I saw your light on in the bakery and also at Thomas Calder's."

"So that would have been about 6:00 a.m.?"

Nora's head tilted. "Maybe a little after since the bendy people were already in the park."

Maddie noted encouragingly. Angel was one of those bendy people and Maddie was sure the class started at 6.30 a.m. in the warmer months.

Mavis tutted. "Why do you get up so early?"

"I like mornings. Always have. You can get a lot done when no one else is about to annoy you," she added pointedly.

"Getting back to your walk," Maddie interrupted. "You didn't see anyone else?"

"No. I walked between the butcher's and the library, crossed the road to the police station, and headed home. Jed was gone by then, but your cat was following me."

If this wasn't so intriguing, Maddie would have laughed. "Did you happen to see a hat outside Thomas's gate?"

"A hat?" Nora looked down her nose. "What kind of hat?"

"Well, a cap really. It was navy blue."

"Not that I recall. I always look ahead to avoid obstacles

and having a fall. It usually spells the end for people my age."

The statement was so firmly delivered that Maddie didn't bother to ask anything more. Just because Nora didn't see the cap didn't mean it wasn't there. For the crime to happen any later didn't make sense. Not with Thomas already at work and with Maddie passing by soon after. So Nora must have been concentrating and hadn't noticed the cap.

Darn it. She hadn't asked Ethan about whether they had found any hairs or other DNA on the cap. Maybe he was waiting until the expert came. Or he was simply keeping any information to himself. Either scenario was plausible.

Chapter Eighteen

Ethan came to the apartment that night looking the worse for wear. Small lines around his eyes had appeared, but he'd showered and wore jeans and a T-shirt.

Maddie was working on the menu, which she put on the side table next to the sofa, and pulled him down beside her. "You look so tired."

"I am and I won't stay long, but I had to see you tonight."

"Because you miss me?" she prompted.

He bent to kiss her before slumping back into the sofa. "Always. Only I have something to say and you're not going to be happy about it."

"Is it to do with Thomas's place?" she asked casually. Perhaps too casually.

Ethan frowned. "No, why do you ask? Or, more to the point, what did you do?"

"Why do you have to assume I'm always up to something?"

The innocent look didn't faze him. "Let's chalk it up to experience."

"Just tell me what's happened."

He sighed. "Rob doesn't want to be my best man if Laura is in the wedding party."

"What?" Her teeth gritted together. "I can't believe he's being so childish."

"Calm down."

He reached for her, but she didn't want to be mollified right now.

"Don't tell me to calm down. How dare he make this all about him."

"He's hurt."

Maddie's anger reached its highest flame and though she knew it wasn't his fault, she considered that Ethan was letting Rob off far too easily. "And so is Laura. Not just at being accused of murder, but by Rob's treatment of her. But this is our wedding. He should appreciate that it's a privilege to be invited to stand beside you and be part of your wedding party. As your friend, he should want to support you, no matter what his feelings are toward Laura. That's what true friends do."

"You're right, but he's not thinking straight. I've never known him to be vindictive and you must see that it's out of character."

"Maybe we don't know him the way we thought we did," she muttered.

"I work with him every day. If he had a dark side, I assure you that I would have noticed it before now. Heck, even Big Red likes him."

That one point got her thinking and Maddie relaxed a little. "I'll concede that does make a difference, but I can't accept that he could pull out of the wedding, and I can't condone how he treated Laura. She needed his support, and I think if he loved her, he could have found a way to be there for her, even with hurt feelings. Even if they aren't more than good friends." She took his hand. "The way you've been there for me."

Ethan smiled and lifted her hand to his lips. "You're worth every drama we've faced, and we'll get through this one together."

Her body tingled as it always did when he touched her, and she managed to smile back. "I wish I had your faith. Right now, as much as I'm upset about Buddy, I'm also worried about the wedding."

"It's hard not to be," he admitted. "However, if anyone can make this work in the time frame, it will be you. Meanwhile, I'll get back to finding the killer, which has to be my major focus right now."

"Of course it is, and that would certainly make everything go smoother."

They stood and held each other tight for a while before he kissed her. When they reluctantly parted, he tapped her nose and waved his set of keys. "No need to see me out."

Holding her fingers to her lips, she waited until he was gone before eyeing Big Red, who watched her from the top of the stairs. "What do you think? Can we do this?" She wasn't entirely sure what she meant because the two issues were both important.

The cat nodded and moved down one step before turning back to face her.

"You want me to follow you? I've got a lot to do. Is it important?" Though she spoke aloud to a cat that couldn't answer, Big Red did have a way of letting her know what he thought, and his demands weren't always about food.

He continued down the steps and waited at the bottom.

When she followed him, he headed to the back door. Since there was a cat flap built into it, he clearly wasn't after a bathroom break. Maddie unlocked the back door and peered outside. There was no sign of Ethan. Grabbing her keys, she locked the door behind her.

"All right, my friend, where are we going?"

Big Red sauntered down Maple Lane. On he went, past the stores and the rear of the library, until he got to the cottage. The porch light was on, and she imagined Gran and Laura sitting at the kitchen table, no doubt having eaten a delicious meal that Maddie could have enjoyed too. The truth was, once she'd found her independence, the desire to hold onto it had meant that living in her own apartment and taking care of herself, rather than letting Gran do everything for her, meant a lot.

Besides, she saw Gran most days and spent hours working alongside her. Evenings could be lonely, but that was before reuniting with her childhood sweetheart. It was nice to spend that time with Ethan, though a nagging thought about how to maintain that independence once he moved in did cause her some anxiety if she allowed it to.

She shook her head and checked to see where Big Red was. The cat sat beside the curb further ahead just out of the shadow of a large maple that, along with a row of them, bordered Gran's farm from the library parking lot. When she got near him, he stood and walked to the edge of the curb and looked pointedly at the road. Something glistened in the moonlight. Maddie knelt down and dabbed her finger on it. The patch was a little sticky right in the middle. Possibly tar, she closed her eyes and sniffed her fingertips.

Blood.

Finding a tissue in her pocket, Maddie wiped her fingers before facing the cottage. She needed to speak to

Laura. Checking her phone for the exact time, she decided it couldn't wait. Gran would understand a late-night visit of this importance.

After knocking, it was Laura who poked her head around the door.

"Oh, it's you."

Maddie could have asked who Laura might have been expecting, but it seemed pretty obvious from the disappointed tone. And interesting. "Sorry to bother you tonight. I'm sure you're exhausted, but I do have a question."

Opening the door wider to let Maddie and Big Red inside, Laura sighed. "I'd be surprised if you didn't."

Gran was in the corner of the sitting room in her special chair that resembled a throne. Putting down her knitting, she gave Big Red a pat before folding her hands in her lap. "What's brought you two out, dear?"

"She's come to interrogate me." Laura shrugged at their surprise. "You left me alone most of the day. I could hear your mind whirring, and I kept hoping you'd put it all together. Did you?" Though she sounded hopeful, Laura's eyes were flat.

Maddie took a seat on the sofa and patted the area beside her. After a brief hesitation, Laura joined her. "I don't have anything concrete yet and neither does Ethan, but he has a specialist coming. All I wanted to ask was how you got home from the bar."

Laura frowned. "Buddy drove me in his car. When I told him it wasn't far to walk, he insisted."

Maddie nodded. "Very gentlemanly. Where did he park?"

"Right out the front of the cottage. Why?" Laura nervously clasped and unclasped her hands, and the way

119

she chewed her lip gave it away that she had something to hide.

"Big Red found some blood on the road. I think it might be where Buddy was killed."

Laura gasped. "But his car wasn't there the next morning, and I heard him leave."

"Did you watch him drive away?"

Laura wrinkled her nose as she considered the question. "I recall waving to him right before I closed the door, and I heard the car start."

"If you didn't see him go, with the door closed, you probably didn't hear the car engine after that?"

"I guess not. Is that important?"

Gran had remained quiet until now. "It could be."

Maddie nodded again. "Knowing where he was killed might be a clue to why Buddy was found in the chiller. Even if it wasn't premeditated. The killer must have been thinking what to do with the body. Maybe they needed time to come to grips with what they'd done and give themselves time to create an alibi. Or maybe they wanted to frame Thomas."

Laura shivered. "This is a nightmare. If only I hadn't agreed to having a meal with Buddy."

"Don't be silly." Gran wagged a finger. "His death had nothing to do with you. If the killer wanted to kill Buddy, then another opportunity would have presented itself."

Laura stood and paced the room twice before she stilled, then faced them again with eyes wide. "What if it was his ex-wife?"

Chapter Nineteen

Maddie blinked at the new information as she tried to absorb it. "I didn't know there was an ex-wife. Did he discuss her with you?"

Laura stood and moved to stand by the unlit fireplace. "He said the marriage had been rocky from the start. They were young and she was impatient that he wasn't famous yet. They separated a few years ago."

It all sounded very convenient, yet what would be the purpose of Buddy lying? Of course, if he was trying to seduce Laura... Maddie kept that thought to herself, as it was a moot point now. "Did you tell Ethan any of this?"

"Of course." Laura's chin dropped to her chest. "I told him everything."

"Not quite everything," Maddie suggested gently.

"You must tell us," Gran insisted as her eyes met Maddie's over Laura's head. "No matter how bad you think it is."

The fact that they had both picked up on Laura's tell convinced Maddie that whatever their friend was hiding was important.

"That's just it. It wasn't bad." Laura's chin tipped up and despite her red cheeks, she said firmly, "I quite liked it. Actually, I liked it a lot."

Her mind going in a direction that made her squirm, Maddie waited with bated breath alongside her wide-eyed Gran for the rest of the revelation.

"Maybe it was because he was so interested in me that I told him about my family. I didn't mean to get upset. Most of the time I can deal with how they basically kicked me out when I wouldn't stay in politics, then left me to fend for myself when I'd never been taught how to do that. Anyway, Buddy hugged me and the next minute we were kissing." Laura covered her face with her hands. "I'm a terrible person."

"There's nothing wrong with that," Gran protested.

"Yes, there is." Laura's voice came out muffled. "You don't kiss someone when you're in love with someone else."

Maddie took her hand and squeezed. "If you love Rob, it wouldn't have happened."

"Oh, Maddie." Gran's mouth turned down as if she were disappointed. "That's not the whole truth of the matter. We can love more than one person in many different ways, and things can happen in the heat of the moment."

Maddie squirmed, a little embarrassed about sounding so black and white, when she already knew that love wasn't as straightforward as she'd once considered. But Gran wasn't done.

"Listen to me—both of you. After you and Ethan fought, Maddie, you left Maple Falls and ended up with Dalton. It was a bad choice, but can you say that when you made it, you didn't still love Ethan?"

Maddie gaped. "I thought I didn't."

"Exactly. Poor Laura has been waiting for Rob to declare his love for so long. Then a man comes onto the scene and gives her everything she needs in that moment to feel alive and wanted. Can you blame her for wanting or taking that moment?"

"Who said I blamed her? I was surprised because—well, because it's Laura." Maddie turned to her friend. "I'm sorry if it seems that way, but I'm certainly not here to judge you. The question is, do you still love Rob after how he's behaved?"

Laura's mouth quivered. "I keep hoping he'll come see me so I can apologize."

"Does he know that you kissed Buddy? I can't see how he could unless you've mentioned it."

Laura's mouth set into a firm line. "Don't you see, if we stand a chance, I have to tell him."

From her high back chair by the fireplace, Gran shrugged. Which said it all. Laura would do things her way and who were they to say if it was right or wrong? The only thing Maddie knew for sure was that Rob wasn't going to be a pushover. Not in the state he was in.

Back at the bakery, Maddie and Big Red sat snuggled up on the bed with a notepad. On it she had made a table with three columns. She labelled column 1, suspects. Column 2 would hold the reasons for their name being there, while column three listed the reasons why they couldn't have killed Buddy.

The first name, for the sake of being fair, was Laura's. She was seen with Buddy and had been with him all evening until late. Her fingerprints were on his belt and his

Stetson. While Gran had heard them outside, only Laura knew when he had presumably left.

Next was Rob. Upset about Laura dating Buddy, was he angry enough to kill his competition? Having seen Laura and Buddy together, had he followed them home and potentially witnessed the kiss? The one Laura had apparently enjoyed a great deal.

After that was Thomas Calder. The butcher's chiller was where the body was found. The men knew each other —or knew of each other. Was it simply due to Buddy being semi-famous in music circles if nothing else? Did Thomas like his music?

Then came the ex-wife. What was her name and where was she now? Obviously, unless she was super strong, she was no more capable of shifting Buddy than Laura. But what if she had help? Or had hired someone else. It seemed a touch outrageous and yet people did terrible things in the name of love, or for money, every day.

Lastly, she'd written *anonymous*. This person may have been one of Buddy's hecklers or perhaps someone upset that the singer had chosen to spend the time after his shows with a young baker.

She tapped her pen on the paper. There was no way she wanted to entertain adding Luke's name to the list. However, the young man was a fan and regardless that he had only ever spoken about Buddy as some kind of hero, he had spent a great deal of time with the singer.

Opening her laptop, she looked up Buddy's ex-wife and got a surprise. The woman had divorced Buddy and married a famous football player soon after. She had no reason to want to harm Buddy when the football player had already amassed a considerable fortune. Unless the new husband wanted to get rid of his wife's past. Permanently.

He could certainly afford to hire someone to do his dirty work, but why bother and risk his career if it got out?

Rubbing her temples, she sighed. If this was the best she could do, they were in trouble. Big Red yawned and stretched so Maddie could rub his stomach, which was oddly soothing for her too.

"We need to find someone who knew Buddy well. Luke might think he does, but he hasn't known him for that long." She snapped her fingers. "We need to go to the bar and find his friends."

She sent a text to the Girlz. "Bachelorette's night, Saturday in Destiny—any takers?"

Angel texted back right away. "Of course! I was going to suggest something, but you seemed to have your hands full with one thing and another."

Maddie laughed at the dig at her sleuthing. Angel wouldn't be surprised when she realized why she'd chosen the bar in Destiny.

Suzy was next. "Thank goodness for a touch of normalcy in this wedding preparation! I'll be there."

Suzy wasn't going to be impressed, but she'd get over it.

Laura's' text was last and not as enthusiastic. "I'll come."

While she could understand her worries, and it wasn't exactly going to be a night they all might expect, Laura needed to get out. Besides, if Maddie was totally honest, Laura might be the only one who could recognize anyone from her date with Buddy if they had been at the bar in Maple Falls that night.

It was a lot of ifs, but to feel like she was doing something helped calm the raging anxiety within her.

Chapter Twenty

The Girlz walked into the bar and stood just inside the doorway. Patrons were scattered around the large room at various tables, and several stood at the bar. At the back was a small stage.

"It's not that busy." Angel noted.

"Really?" Laura scoffed. "There are heaps of people here."

"Compared to Maple Falls, sure. But not for Destiny. I guess we're a little early."

"Any later and it'll be my bedtime," Laura muttered.

Angel laughed. "Sugar, you need to relax a little. There are some cute guys in here."

Laura shifted uncomfortably and turned away while Suzy wrinkled her nose.

"If you like that hairy look."

"You know I do." Angel nudged the much shorter woman. "Let out that wild child for a change."

"School principals don't have a wild child side to them." Suzy sniffed. "Not if they want to keep their job."

"Oh, sugar, you must have forgotten that Maddie and I

knew you back when. You knew how to have a good time, and don't you deny it."

"I guess I had my moments, but I have to behave myself these days."

Laura studied the posters on the wall beside them and suddenly grabbed Maddie's arm. "Tell me this isn't the bar that Buddy sang in."

Her stomach did a deep dive and Maddie could only nod. "Actually, this is where Luke met him."

Laura stiffened and dropped her arm as if burned. "I can't stay here."

One look at her friend's face and Maddie knew she had made a big mistake. "I'm so sorry. What a terrible friend I am."

Suzy's nostrils flared. "Wait one darn minute. We're here on false pretenses—this isn't your bachelorette's night?"

Maddie nodded, deeply ashamed. "All I was thinking about was finding Buddy's killer and I figured that person might have been someone from here. Of course we should go."

"I should have known you wouldn't actually want a bachelorette's party, and Laura's right; you should have told her about Buddy singing here." Angel waved a hand around the room. "However, if you can stomach it, Laura, this might be the only chance to find out who he knew that had a grudge against him. Plus, it couldn't hurt to have a bite to eat and a drink. It's not like you saw him perform or anything, is it?"

Angel had a way about her that was a mix of kindness, tough love, and coercion. Right now with her arm around Laura's shoulders, it was hard to tell which was having the most effect. Maddie held her breath.

Eventually, Laura rubbed a hand over her pale face. "Since we're here anyway, I guess it couldn't hurt."

"Only if you're sure it won't upset you?" No matter that she wanted a chance to find someone who knew something, Maddie would leave if Laura said the word.

Laura shrugged. "You should know by now that the only thing I'm sure about is baking."

"That's our girl." Angel squeezed her shoulder. "Brave even when you don't want to be."

While Laura rolled her eyes, the corners of her mouth gave a hint of a smile and Maddie turned to Suzy. "What do you think?"

"Fine." She huffed. "We'll get a table, and you can buy the darn drinks, Sherlock."

Maddie went to the bar with mixed feelings. While grateful for Angel's intervention and Laura's change of heart, the guilt lingered. Dragging her friend out on false pretenses, when she clearly hadn't wanted to go to a place that might upset her, wasn't the sort of thing she usually did. What kind of person was she turning into? She barely acknowledged the man taking her order and once back at the table she apologized again.

Laura hushed her by laying a hand over hers. "I overreacted. As Angel said, this bar means nothing to me and nor do these people. I admit it was a shock, and you know how I hate those." She shrugged. "It may seem that I'm hiding from what happened, but I swear, I want his killer found as much as you."

"We never doubted it," Angel assured her, and the others nodded.

Laura sighed. "It's just that I have this feeling of guilt that I can't shake."

"What do you have to feel guilty for?" Suzy demanded.

"And don't go spouting that 'if you hadn't gone on a date with Buddy' nonsense. Let's get real here. There is someone out there who had a beef with the singer, which had nothing to do with you. They were bent on killing him no matter who he was with."

"That may be true, but he was with me, and I can't forget that." Laura dipped her head. "And then there's Rob."

This admission made more sense to Maddie. Buddy had showered Laura with oodles of attention, something her friend had never experienced. Rob was friendly, but certainly not attentive. Naturally, Laura had been flattered, which had perhaps made it easier to forget about the attachment she felt to Rob—for a short time.

"Don't you feel bad about him and his hurt feelings." Suzy wagged a finger at Laura. "If he's not man enough to fight for you, then he's not man enough for you, period."

Angel nodded. "The way he treated you was out of line, and if nothing else good comes from this tragedy, then maybe it will be that he realizes his mistake."

Before Laura could comment, a different barman brought their drinks. Middle-aged, he wore jeans and a plaid shirt, which strained at the buttons over his belly. "Good evening. It's not often we get a group of such lovely-looking ladies in here. What brings you to Barney's?"

The broad smile seemed genuine, and Maddie decided a barman was a good place to start with any questions. "We're on a bachelorette's night, but I was also hoping to talk to someone about Buddy Preston."

His face fell. "Aww, I'm sorry to tell you, but he passed a few days back."

"Yes, we heard. It's very sad. We're actually from Maple Falls where we recently met him. I'm Maddie Flynn. This is Angel, Laura, and Suzy. It's so hard to believe he's gone. Do you know if anyone here had a problem with him?"

"Pleased to meet you. Name's Hugo. Let me tell you that it came as a terrible shock. As far as I know, everybody loved Buddy."

"Not quite everyone," Suzy muttered. "You do know he was murdered?"

"Murdered?" Hugo's eyes widened for only a moment. "No one said that outright. Though I did figure that's what happened after all the questions."

Maddie leaned forward eagerly. "Someone else has been asking about him?"

"Sure. The police came by the next day and spoke to a lot of people in here."

"Of course they did, but what I meant was did anyone else other than the police come by to ask questions?"

"Not that I recall. We have several staff to cover the hours. More of us work on Friday and Saturday nights when it's busiest."

"I see. Getting back to the police, I take it that no one was taken in for questioning?"

"Not from here, or I would have heard about it. And I haven't heard about anyone in town being arrested either."

Suzy smirked. "I'm thinking in your job, you would hear all the goings on around town."

He chuckled. "You have no idea what people tell a barman and I'm here most nights."

"It looks like a nice bar," Angel noted.

He nodded. "Best I've ever worked in. I enjoy the music, and the crowd is friendly enough."

"Are there shows other than Saturday nights?" Maddie asked.

"Shows are mainly on Friday and Saturday, unless it's a

holiday." He nodded to the opposite corner of the room. The jukebox is usually going the rest of the time."

"You say the crowd is friendly." Maddie toyed with her straw. "Has there ever been any issues?"

"You mean fights? People sure do like a good debate around here." He chuckled again.

That could mean so many different things, and Maddie decided to press a little more. "Has there been anything that could have led to wanting to pay somebody back for a perceived slight."

"Well, I can't rightly say. Most arguments are over and done within a short time. Whenever it gets heated, we send the hot-head home, and the next time they turn up, it's never been a big deal. Barney, he's the owner, don't like nobody getting too riled. The regulars know if you overstep, you ain't getting back in after he kicks you out. Not that night or any other."

"That's strict for such a big town." Suzy nodded approvingly. "I wish more bars were like that."

"It works, and now that I'm getting older, throwing people out isn't appealing, nor much of an option." Hugo winked. "Plus, I like knowing this place is safe. That's why it's hard to consider anyone here wanting to hurt Buddy." With a glance over his shoulder, he picked up the empty tray. "I'm getting an evil look from Barney, so I best get back behind the bar. Nice to make your acquaintance."

"Nice to meet you, too, Hugo, and thanks for taking the time to talk to us." Maddie watched him walk back to the bar. The customers seemed to like him, and he got several pats on the shoulder as he maneuvered his way around the tables.

Angel took a sip of her cocktail. "Mmmm, this is so good. What a lovely man."

"A lovely man with no answers. Looks like a dead end to me." Suzy took a sip, then grinned. "But you're right. Darned if this cocktail isn't worth the drive."

Back at the bar, the man who must be the owner looked to be giving Hugo a stern word. Maddie hoped they hadn't caused trouble by detaining him so long.

Chapter Twenty-One

It wasn't long before the band arrived and began setting up in the corner. The place was beginning to fill, and the bar was busy.

"Can we order food now?" Angel had been perusing the menu practically from the minute they sat down. "If we don't get our orders in soon, we'll be waiting a long while and I'm starving."

"I could eat." Suzy lifted her empty glass. "And how about another cocktail?"

Maddie raised an eyebrow at Laura, who nodded. "Tell me what you want, and I'll order it when I get fresh drinks."

Armed with the list of food, she deliberately waited until Hugo was free before approaching the bar. "Could we get another round of three of the same cocktails and one mocktail, please?"

With a grin, Hugo took the food list and keyed it into a tablet. "Someone's organized. You the sober driver?"

"That's right."

"Mocktail's on the house, then. We like to promote safe driving."

"What a fantastic idea. I should tell the owner of our bar in Maple Falls about that policy. Do you mind if I ask you another couple of questions while you're making the drinks?"

He checked on the whereabouts of his boss, who was over by the band. "Go right ahead."

"I wonder if you recall a young man who got friendly with Buddy? He's fair-haired, lanky, and rather quiet."

Hugo nodded. "Yeah, I do. Luke somebody?"

"That's right." She beamed. "He's a friend of ours and he came here a lot."

"He sure did. Once he got in tight with Buddy, he was here most nights. I couldn't figure out what they had in common, but they talked for hours. Eric seemed a bit put out about it at first, but like the rest of us, he could see that the kid was good for Buddy."

Maddie's skin tingled. "Eric?"

"Yeah, he and Buddy go way back. Before your friend arrived on the scene, Eric and Buddy were inseparable."

"Is he here tonight?"

"Let me see?" Hugo glanced around the room. "He hasn't been in for a while. Oh, wait. There he is, in the corner."

Even sitting, it was obvious that Eric was a large man. "Would you mind introducing me to him?"

"Sure, but don't be surprised if he's not chatty. After all, he's mourning his friend."

Hugo loaded the tray, and she followed him over to Eric. The man glanced up at Maddie as she approached. Oddly, his eyes widened for a moment before he dropped his gaze and went back to nursing his beer.

"This little lady would like to meet you, Eric."

This time Eric gave her a longer look. "I'm not buying anything."

Maddie raised an eyebrow. "That's fine. I'm not selling anything. Though maybe I should be offended?"

"He didn't mean nothing by that," Hugo said quickly.

Eric stiffened. "Don't speak for me, Hugo."

"Then don't be rude. Costs nothing to hear her out, unless you have something important to do."

Hugo's tone held disbelief, which was interesting, as was Eric's response.

"One day you're going to say too much."

Maddie didn't like the glint in Eric's eyes. "Look, I haven't come to stir up trouble. I just wanted to know if you can think of a reason why Buddy Preston was murdered?"

"And what the heck has that, and what I know or don't know, got to do with you?" he growled.

"So you do know something," Maddie pressed.

"That's not what I said. Now, go away," he growled deeper.

Maddie stood her ground, convinced Eric knew something. "Don't you want the killer to be brought to justice? I thought Buddy was your friend?"

"Best friend I ever had." A tic in his jaw made him speak through clenched teeth. "Why do you care so much?" His eyes narrowed. "You don't look like a cop."

"I'm not." She nodded across the room. "My friend over there, the one with the red hair, was with him earlier the night he died. She can't get over it until she knows why it happened. I only met him once, but I feel the same way."

"She says she's a friend of Luke's," Hugo offered.

Eric downed the rest of his beer and stood to tower over her. "Buddy was in a mess a while back. His greedy wife left him for someone with money and he couldn't handle it.

He started smoking weed like there was no tomorrow and that meant he lost gigs and friends. Then Luke came along, and he was good for Buddy. He stopped smoking altogether and settled on a beer or two at most. Soon, Barney offered him a regular spot." The big man then muttered, "He was the happiest I saw him in a long while."

Now that he was standing, there was something about Eric that seemed familiar and yet she didn't recognize his face. "Do you know what he and Luke spoke about?"

"Best you ask your friend," he growled. "After a while I got bored with the two of them jawing on about old times and fathers who weren't worth a darn. As long as Buddy was happy, I didn't have to watch over him." He looked away. "I'm sorry I stopped."

Maddie could almost feel his pain and something else rolling off him in waves. "Have you ever been to Maple Falls."

Eric eyed the door. "I rarely leave Destiny. Small towns don't appeal to me."

While she imagined plenty of people felt this way, Maddie wasn't sure he was being entirely truthful. "I see. Well thanks for speaking to me."

"Can't imagine it helps much." Eric touched a finger to his forehead, grabbed a battered Stetson from beside him and marched out of the bar as if he couldn't wait to get away from her.

Nothing was any clearer, but Eric had at least confirmed that Buddy had issues. Plus an ex-wife who wanted more. "Thanks for the introduction, Hugo."

"Not sure it helped any, but it was my pleasure. I was fond of Buddy." They walked back to the girlz and Hugo handed out the drinks. "Better get yourself seated. The band's about to start and your food won't be long."

"What have you been up to, and why did that big man look upset when he left?" Angel demanded as soon as they were alone.

"According to Hugo, that was Buddy's best friend."

"Really?" Laura asked. "What did he say?"

Maddie told them and watched Laura's horrified reaction.

"Buddy was a drug user?"

"That's what Eric said, but he also said that he was reformed."

Laura shook her head sadly. "It's all so unbelievable. Like you're talking about someone else."

Suzy took a large gulp of her drink. "Look, I don't want to be the bad guy here, but you have to quit thinking you knew the man. At best, it was twelve hours. He had a lifetime of living behind him that shaped who he was. Knowing a few things is just a drop in the ocean. You can't appreciate the context of what the big guy said, so you will never know who Buddy really was before you met him."

Laura blinked at her. "You aren't the bad guy, and I hear you. Only, he was the first man I ever kissed properly."

The air whooshed out of Suzy like a whoopee cushion with no joy. "You're serious, aren't you? Sheesh, what the heck is wrong with Rob?"

Laura took a long drink. "The thing is, I've been wondering all this time what was wrong with me."

"Don't you ever think that," Suzy growled. "You are a beautiful woman. Rob's the idiot here. The man clearly has no clue about the birds and the bees."

Maddie choked on her mocktail and had to clean herself up while the other two commiserated with Laura.

"This is shocking, and I'm so sad that you couldn't have

known Buddy better, sugar, but at least you now know how desirable you are."

"Thank you, Angel. For a moment, I truly did feel that way. Maybe that's why I'm so confused about how things were with Rob and the guilt over enjoying the attention."

"Guilt is overrated and the kind you're talking about is a waste of time." Suzy slapped her hand on the tabletop. "Who wouldn't take a kiss from a cute singer, especially when your supposed boyfriend isn't interested?"

Maddie kicked Suzy under the table.

"Ouch! I only meant that we have to take what we need sometimes and at thirty that includes, at the very least, a kiss."

Angel shrugged. "She's not wrong, sugar. In fact, most women have to kiss a lot of frogs before they get themselves a prince."

"That's the problem. Where are all the frogs?" Laura suddenly smirked and then they were laughing.

Maddie felt a slight ease in her stomach. Though it would take some time, Laura was slowly on the way to healing. They'd discovered more about their friend, which helped to understand her better and made the Girlz an even tighter unit. Maybe this bachelorette's night wasn't such a bust after all.

Chapter Twenty-Two

The band consisted of two singers, who played guitars, and a drummer. They were pretty good and before long the Girlz were tapping their feet.

"Maybe you could ask them if they're free to play at your wedding?" Suzy suggested.

Maddie shook her head. "This bar is about the same size as the community center, if you take in the pool tables and dance floor. I think they'd be too loud."

"I'm so glad you think so," Laura yelled a little unnecessarily. "My ears are ringing."

Maddie leaned into her. "I'm sorry. As soon as we've eaten, we can get out of here."

"I don't want to spoil your bachelorette's night," Laura protested.

"I'm hardly a party girl." Maddie gave a wry grin. "What with being up so early Monday to Saturday, any extra sleep is a bonus."

Done with her meal, Angel jumped to her feet when a young man asked her to dance. "It's been a while since I heard this kind of music, and I aim to make the most of it until y'all are ready."

"Look at her go," Suzy remarked with a touch of envy.

"Why don't you dance too?" Maddie nudged her. "I bet if you made eye contact with one of the guys looking at you, instead of being all unapproachable, they'd be over like a shot."

"I'm fine right here. They're all too young or too old."

"You sure you're not too fussy?"

"Maybe," Suzy conceded. "I just want to enjoy this night with my friends. It might be the last one for a while— once you're married."

Suzy was a good friend, and though she could be forth-right, she was always there when needed to help in any way she could. If she wasn't interested in dancing, that was fine with Maddie, who didn't feel like it either. She put an arm around Suzy's shoulder and did the same with Laura. "I'll always have time for my Girlz."

"You heard her." Suzy grinned at Laura. "It's our job to ensure she keeps her promise."

Laura grinned back. "I accept the challenge."

A light behind Laura's eyes had come back on. It burned brighter than it had for a while, and Maddie hoped it would continue to do so after the cocktails had worn off and they were back in Maple Falls.

A while later, when they had finished their burgers and drinks, Laura leaned back and yawned. Seeing her cue, Maddie stood. "Ready when you are. Though I might need help getting the belle of the ball out of here."

Suzy put two fingers in her mouth and whistled. The place stopped dead except for the music.

Angel waved over her dance partner's head, said something in his ear, and then joined them. "You're such a classy principal."

"I know." Suzy threw back her head of curls and sauntered out the door.

The drive home was lively as they joked about the series of men Angel had danced with.

"I swear that last one wasn't twenty." Angel snorted. "He was all over me, asking for my number and address. I had to stop a minute and give the boy some advice."

Bug-eyed, Laura leaned closer to the passenger seat. "What kind of advice?"

Angel put up a finger. "Don't touch a woman unless it's a slow dance—and she says yes. Don't beg for anything. Listen to your partner and don't fill every second with talking. Sometimes people just want to dance. Copy the best dancers so you don't look like one of those air-dancers outside a car sales yard."

By the time all fingers were in the air, Suzy and Laura were hysterical in the back seat.

"What did he say?" Laura hiccupped.

"He thanked me kindly and went and hid in the corner. I guess his confidence was rocked, but hopefully, he'll take some of it onboard for next time."

"One can only hope." Suzy giggled. "Did you have a good time, Maddie?"

"I did, thanks to you three."

"We do make a good team." Angel faced her. "Though I'm sorry you didn't get all the information you wanted."

"It's fine. Being with my friends was the best part of the night and should always have been the focus. Though I admit, talking to Eric was enlightening, so I feel like I did get something out of it from that perspective." Maddie nodded in the rearview mirror. "However, we're still no closer to finding the killer, and I'd say it actually added the possibility for more suspects."

Angel tilted her head. "If it was premeditated, then they could have had a grudge—like Eric missing time with his friend. Or a rival band wanting his spot."

"Exactly, but I'm not sure about the premeditation angle," Maddie muttered almost to herself.

"How did you come to that conclusion?" Angel pressed. "Was it the blood on the road?"

"What are you talking about?" Suzy demanded. "I thought we had all the details and blood on the road doesn't ring any bells."

"I found the blood when I went to see Laura and I can't shake the feeling that Buddy knew his killer. The fact that neither Gran nor Laura heard any noise, makes sense if the killer got into the vehicle and then attacked Buddy. When he tried to escape, he could have fallen out and onto the road, which would explain the blood on the ground where the driver's door potentially was. Hopefully, Ethan will have had it analyzed by now."

"That's a lot of possibles and could haves, but nothing concrete," Suzy noted.

Maddie nodded. "So many possibles and things I never thought to ask before. Like where is Buddy's car? Whether Buddy was killed in his car or not, there must be blood on the inside of it."

"Not if your guesswork isn't what actually happened," Suzy said reasonably.

"True, but there was definitely blood on Thomas's back door and on that cap I found. I also wonder where the killer's vehicle was at the time of the murder. Assuming that the killer was from out of town supports my thoughts of there being more than one person responsible," Maddie explained.

"Two killers?"

"Or one and an assistant. Think about it. The killer couldn't drive two vehicles. Buddy's car wasn't in sight when I got to Thomas's. There had to be two people, or the killer ran the risk of getting caught if he first removed Buddy's car and then came back for his own."

"Well doesn't that fly in the face of your idea of it not being premeditated?"

Maddie blinked. "You're right, Angel. They would have had to have a plan which included following Buddy to Gran's and would mean that the getaway vehicle couldn't be too far away."

"Unless the killer was dropped off and the other person went to the pickup point."

"Good thinking, Laura. Still, Buddy wasn't a small man. Someone of your build couldn't have moved him out of the vehicle and into Thomas's. Even a bigger person would have struggled with, excuse me, a dead weight."

Angel shivered. "The idea of two people involved makes it seem a lot worse. If that's possible."

"I agree. But if that is the case, where did they take the car? Or did they hide it in Maple Falls?"

"Why would they hide it in Maple Falls?" Laura scoffed. "I mean, where could they hide it without someone finding it pretty fast?

"Are you kidding me? We have farmland all around the town," Angel said dryly.

Maddie stared at her. "Oh my gosh! Why didn't I think of that? Gran's fields are right across the road from the stores. We need to look for tire tracks."

"Not tonight!" Angel protested.

Maddie laughed as she parked Honey in the garage. "Not tonight. Even with a flashlight, it would be difficult. Besides if we blundered around the fields, we'd most likely destroy any evidence."

Angel snorted. "With the amount of alcohol in those cocktails, blundering is about all you'd get from me right now."

"How about we meet up tomorrow morning?" Laura suggested as they walked up the path to the bakery kitchen.

The others gaped at her sudden change of heart.

"What? I might not like everything that's happened over the last few days, but I did say that I want Buddy's murder solved. You could all come to the cottage and after we've checked out the fields, I'll make breakfast."

A noise up ahead got their attention. "And what exactly would you four be checking the fields for?"

Laura squealed and Suzy swung her purse at the shadow near the door as the sensor light flicked on.

Chapter Twenty-Three

"It's okay. It's Ethan," Maddie yelled, unsure who was more surprised by the reaction of her friends—she or Ethan.

"Sheesh! Way to give us a heart attack," Suzy grumbled as she allowed her purse to fall harmlessly.

"Sorry, I didn't mean to scare you, but I would like an answer about the fields."

"Don't you want to know if Maddie enjoyed herself?" Angel asked in a tight voice.

Ethan folded his arms over his chest. "How did the bachelorette's night go?"

Obviously, he'd heard enough to be aware of what they had planned but decided to humor them. Maddie played along, glad to have the Girlz there to defuse the situation. "We had a great time at Barney's in Destiny."

His eyes narrowed. "I wonder why you didn't tell me that's where you were headed. Could it be because that's where Buddy Preston performed?"

"That was part of the reason," Maddie admitted. "The

music is very good though. We should go there one night. It'll be fun."

"I'm sure." Sarcasm dripped off the words. "And what did you do while you were there?"

"Angel danced her feet off." Maddie laughed unnaturally.

"And you, my innocent fiancée, what did you do?"

She licked her lips. "I watched the dancing and chatted to some people."

"Of course you did. Anyone I might know?"

"Hey, why don't we head home and let the two of you chat?" Angel was already walking down the path to the gate. Suzy and Laura hurried after her.

"I guess my bachelorette's night is over," Maddie told him wryly as she unlocked the door and went inside.

He didn't follow her. "It didn't have to be over. Sorry if I broke it up early. Just thought I'd stop by and make sure you got home safe."

His worry for her was there in the furrowed brow. "It's fine. I'd had enough partying for one night, but I'd love you to come in if you have some time?"

"I'm on duty. Still, I wouldn't say no to a hot drink—and some answers."

She grimaced and hurried upstairs where Big Red was stretched along the sofa. "Make some room, buddy," she called to him, and immediately regretted it. That name would have a different meaning for some time. Flicking on the smaller version of the coffee maker from downstairs, Maddie made him a long black and a decaf for herself to avoid being up all night.

When they were seated on the sofa with Big Red between them, Ethan took a careful gulp before turning to her.

"Ready to tell me what you were up to?"

The time to make the coffees had helped settle her nerves and she merely nodded before relaying the evening including her conversation with Eric.

He digested the information for several heartbeats. "That's interesting. No one of that name was there when we were interviewing the staff and the owner didn't mention him."

"Eric's not a staff member," she explained. "He's Buddy's best friend. Or was."

"I meant Hugo."

Maddie blinked. "Now that is odd, because he told me about the police coming to interview everyone. It never occurred to me to ask Hugo if he'd been interviewed. I just assumed he had been."

"Did you get a last name?"

"Sorry, that didn't occur to me either," she groaned, annoyed with herself.

Ethan frowned, deep in thought for a moment. "I think I'd better pay Barney's another visit."

"Can I ask you a question?"

"You can always ask."

She smiled, though she got the inference that he didn't have to answer and probably wouldn't. "Did you happen to notice blood on the road in front of the cottage?"

"We did," he said slowly.

"Excellent. Do you know what happened to Buddy's car?"

"That's two questions."

"Do you think it was more than one person involved, because I do."

Ethan drained his cup. "I'm not saying anything more

about the case. I promise, we are working on it, so how about letting it go and concentrating on other things?"

"Such as?"

"Anything not case-related. Perhaps the wedding?"

The pointed suggestion had some merit. Still... "Our wedding will be a liability if anything happens."

"I agree, but we can't be held to ransom by a ghost."

She nodded. "We need to find the killer in the next few days."

"I am trying. Now you've deflected enough. What about this field business?"

Maddie thought he'd forgotten and couldn't hold back. "That's all to do with the missing car. If it was outside Gran's and you don't have it impounded, then where did it go?"

"Maybe he sold it."

"The killer?"

"No. A friend of Buddy's."

"You're making no sense. Buddy died and his car disappeared."

"Or did it?"

Her eyes widened. "You're toying with me."

"No, I'm trying to make you see that there could be so many scenarios here and I don't need you muddying the waters by contaminating my crime scenes."

"Right. So, you do think that the farm could be a part of this? Perhaps where the car was hidden?"

"Wow." He stood and stretched. "I'm getting out of here."

She stood too. "Don't say it like that. I really do love you."

"Too easy, Maddie. And too obvious."

"That doesn't make it less true."

He pulled her into his arms and kissed the top of her head. "I know. I just hate for you to think I'm a pushover."

"Ditto. But you knew that about me."

"I sure did. Until the day you up and left Maple Falls, I still thought I could talk you into staying. I was young and such an idiot."

"We both were. When I told you I had to go to try something new and find myself, you said some mean things."

"As I recall, we both did. Yours was something about me being bossy, a chauvinist, predictable, and boring. I might have missed a couple more." He winked. "I guess it was supposed to happen this way."

She ran a hand down his cheek, brushing the thickening stubble. "So we'd know how far to push each other and what love really meant."

"Exactly." He leaned down and kissed her sweetly. "And I wouldn't change a thing."

"You say that now," she teased.

"True. Tomorrow might be a different story if you ignore everything I've said."

"I would never ignore everything," she promised.

His chest rumbled and she smiled into the side of his neck. They didn't have to agree on everything or like it, but they did understand and accept each other for who they were.

Chapter Twenty-Four

Unable to sleep, Maddie got out of bed the next morning and after a quick wash, traipsed downstairs. Baking helped to ease her mind and also let it expand the possibilities. This was how she refined a recipe and worked out how to improve it or discard it if it turned out to not be a viable option.

Despite it being Sunday, the honey cake was getting another iteration. That didn't mean that she couldn't focus on other things. In fact, it was the opposite and just what she needed. Last night had opened up new motives. Ones she imagined Ethan was already eliminating.

A longtime friend who had been set aside for Luke; Eric had to be a strong suspect. What about Hugo? The friendly barman seemed so open, but had he deliberately avoided the police when they went to the bar, or was that just a coincidence? Angel had also made a remark that nagged at Maddie. What if the band which had been ousted from their usual slot, and replaced with Buddy, were indeed angry over the slight? Then there was the drugs angle.

While she didn't want to make a big deal about it when

Laura had been so horrified, Suzy was right about none of them knowing Buddy properly—not Laura, and not even Luke who had spent the most time with him. Their contact had been limited to the bar and even if they weren't drinking, it wasn't like hanging out on a daily basis or seeing people outside of their comfort zone.

A quick rap at the door and Angel entered, Big Red at her heels. The cat slunk through the small hall and went upstairs.

"You two are up early."

Maddie wiped her hands on a towel and placed the pan of batter in the oven. "I could say the same for you. Usually, I have to throw something at your window on a Sunday. Are you worried about the murder?"

Angel sighed. "To be honest, I'm equal parts worried about that and nervous about the wedding. I'd hoped the bachelorette's night might have helped all of us, but as much fun as it was, the murder does affect everything. You didn't get very far with any clues, did you?"

Maddie shrugged. "Not really, but we did find out more about Buddy, which can only help. I'm hopeful something will turn up soon."

Angel ran a finger around the dirty bowl and popped a little batter into her mouth. "Mmm. That's good. What did the handsome sheriff have to say about the bachelorette's night?"

"He wasn't at all happy about it and warned me off going to Gran's to check the fields."

Angel's eyebrows rose. "And?"

"We won't go into the fields," Maddie insisted, "but if we look over the fence across the road—the whole paddock long—and we take a look through Gran's kitchen window. Maybe we'll see if it's a dead end or find it's a loose strand."

"I like that idea. Plus, I'm already hungry and Laura did promise us breakfast."

Maddie rolled her eyes. "Suzy's not here yet and I need another thirty minutes for the cake to finish baking."

Angel groaned. "Couldn't we check out the fields across the road to kill time now? Then we won't have to do it later."

"Great idea." Maddie whipped off her apron, and after closing the door behind her, they went across the road. There was no footpath here and they had to walk through long grass to get to the fence. Maddie climbed to the top rail and swung her legs over so that she was sitting on it. Angel followed suit and they stared out over the long pasture. The grass here had been eaten down and a few cows ambled their way toward them.

"Should we get down?" Angel asked nervously.

"They're just curious."

"Yeah, but they are pretty big, sugar."

Maddie laughed. "You've been around farm animals most of your life. Why are you suddenly nervous around these?"

"I think you mistook my happiness about being included in your family for a love of livestock. I was never that comfortable."

"Hah! You learn something new every day." Maddie's eyes narrowed. "Speaking of which. Look over there. Is that what I think it is?"

"Tire tracks!" Angel squealed.

"Yep. See how the maple trees cover both sides of the fence? Whoever drove the car in here must have scratched the paintwork."

"You haven't said if the police ever found Buddy's car."

"Ethan hasn't mentioned it. Though I'm pretty sure he

wouldn't." Maddie's eyes widened. "Especially if it was a major piece of evidence."

"Oooh. So they may have found the car and have it locked up somewhere."

Maddie nodded and almost fell off her perch when Big Red launched himself at her ankle. "What's going on with you?"

The ginger ball meowed angrily and ran back to the road.

"What's his problem?" Angel asked.

"I'm not sure, but I aim to find out." After scrambling down, Maddie ran across the road and followed Big Red into the bakery. The oven door stood open, blasting hot air into the room. The cake inside was ruined.

"How did that happen?" Angel peered over her shoulder. "I'm sure the door was closed."

"It was. Maybe the lock gave way." Maddie jiggled it, then opened and closed the door several times. "I don't understand."

"Hey, what's up with Big Red?" Suzy called from the doorway as she looked behind her.

"What do you mean?" Maddie asked.

"He completely ignored me and raced up the street like he was after a rat."

Maddie faced Angel. "Do you think it's possible that someone came in here while we were across the road?"

Her friend paled. "Come to think of it, I closed the back door when we left and it was open when we came back."

Maddie blinked. "That's right. I saw you do it. And I know that I closed the oven door."

Suzy came inside and immediately picked up on the vibe. "What's going on here?"

"To be honest, I'm not sure," Maddie admitted. "Would

there be any way for the back door to open and in turn cause the oven door to open? Or vice versa?"

Suzy frowned. "You two are scaring me."

Angel explained the situation then Suzy immediately checked both doors with the other two watching closely.

"I can't see how the two doors opening could possibly be related. When the back door is closed, it's firm and even pushing on it doesn't make it open. Same thing happens when I bang the oven's door and sides."

"Thanks, Suzy. That means that someone was in here and I think Big Red saw them." Maddie turned off the oven and removed the cake from it. I'm going to see where he went."

Angel and Suzy shared a look and nodded. "Okay. Let's go."

Maddie didn't answer. Right before she'd turned off the oven something had fluttered by her feet. She crouched to study it and the others peered over her shoulder.

"What did you find?" Suzy asked.

Maddie sighed. "It's only a feather."

"Eww. Has Big Red been catching birds?"

Angel snorted. "With the way he gets feed by everyone there's no need for that kind of exercise."

Maddie stood and hurried to the door. "He wouldn't do that, and since he's probably chasing down whoever was in here, I don't think you should poke fun at him. We better hurry."

Chapter Twenty-Five

The three women hurried out of the gate and turned right. At the corner, they stopped.

Maddie looked left and right and then across the road to the green and beyond. "They'll be well out of sight if they went into the trees at the back of the park. Let's walk up to the corner of Main Street."

The two corners were only the length of the stores plus their gardens in width so it only took a few seconds. While there were several people on the streets, it was a Sunday and therefore quiet. Big Red was nowhere to be seen, left, right, or straight ahead.

"We wasted precious time checking out the doors," Angel moaned.

"It couldn't be helped. We didn't appreciate what had happened until we did," Maddie assured her, though she was just as frustrated.

"It's a bit cheeky breaking in during broad daylight when you were just across the road."

Maddie grabbed her friend and squeezed. "Suzy, you're brilliant!

"Huh?"

"They were cheeky," Maddie explained, "but if they waited until we were back inside the bakery, then they had time to get in and get away without being seen." She pointed across the road. "Providing they went via the park."

"Yes!" Angel pumped a fist. "You cracked it."

"Not yet," she reminded her. "Not until I find them. You two head to the station. Ethan should be there, but if not, tell whoever is on duty what's going on."

Angel grabbed Maddie's arm as she turned to go across the road. "No way are you chasing them down on your own."

Maddie hesitated for a second. "I have to go if we stand any chance of not losing them."

"It's too dangerous." Suzy sided with Angel.

"Not if I'm careful. I promise not to take any unnecessary risks."

Angel pouted. "That's the problem—you never seem to know what that means."

"Please," Maddie implored. "I have to find out who killed Buddy for all our sakes. If I don't go now, then they may get away."

"Maybe, but they'll be back if this is all a way of getting you to stop what you're doing."

"Exactly. And what might their next attempt look like? We can't let them get away with this."

Angel sighed heavily. "Fine. Suzy, you go to the station and I'll go with Maddie."

"You don't need to," Maddie objected.

"Yeah, I do, sugar. I couldn't live with myself if something happened to you. Plus, I have a beautiful dress to wear in a week and nothing's going to stop your wedding if I can prevent it."

Reluctantly, Suzy hurried down Main Street while Maddie and Angel ran across the road and then across the green.

Angel came to a stop at the edge of the woods. "This is all good, but which way?"

Maddie stopped too and searched the area around them. "We can rule out the walkway into the other end of Main Street."

"How do you know?"

Maddie pointed to a shrub beside her where strands of ginger fluff fluttered in the slight breeze. "Big Red went that way."

"Clever cat. Let's go!" Angel led the charge.

Running as fast as the tree trunks allowed, they emerged into a small clearing and another entrance to the main road. Big Red sat at the edge of the grass verge and gave them a surly glance before staring down the street.

"Where did they go?" Angel rasped.

"I think he's trying to tell us." Maddie pointed at the grass. "Tire tracks lead onto the road."

"I'd bet good money that these are the same as the ones in Gran's field."

Maddie shook her head. "I'm afraid you'd lose. These are motorcycle tracks. It looks like four tires because they've driven in and turned around when they left." Disappointment turned to anxiety when she heard a siren. Despite being glad that the police could get onto the case right away, she knew Ethan wasn't going to be happy. Especially after their very recent conversation.

Sure enough, it was Ethan who stormed out of the car. "Are you both okay?"

"Yes, we didn't find anyone." Maddie pointed. "But Big Red thinks they went down that way."

His nostrils flared and it wasn't through any disbelief over a cat having an opinion. He'd known Big Red for as long as Maddie and had witnessed his talent first-hand many times. No, he was so angry with Maddie.

"Chasing after a criminal was a dangerous and irresponsible thing to do. Don't you want to get married?"

"Of course I do. That's why I can't have this hanging over our heads. If we don't get the mystery solved soon, we might have to postpone the wedding."

"How many times do we have to go back and forth over this? Buddy's death has likely nothing to do with the wedding."

"Being likely as opposed to definitely not, isn't enough to satisfy my fears."

Ethan shook his head. "I just don't know what to do or say that will make you see reason."

"I'm sorry. Only, I can't help how I feel. Did you hear that they were in the bakery? In broad daylight!"

"Suzy told me all about it. I can't talk to you right now, as I have to follow your cat's instructions. For pity's sake, go home and stay there." With another shake of his head, he rammed his hat back on and marched back to the car.

Angel took her arm and led her away. This time, they walked around the road.

Suzy waited by the gate. "Ethan wasn't impressed."

"No, he wasn't." For the first time ever, Maddie didn't want to go back into the bakery. "Let's go to Gran's as we intended."

The quiver in her voice must have been apparent and her friends walked one on each side keeping quiet, but she saw the look pass between them. They were worried, too, and she felt so responsible. Yet, what could she have done differently?

Laura met them at the door. "I've had the breakfast made for an hour."

"Sorry. It's been a morning." Maddie went down the hall and slumped in a chair at the kitchen table.

"What's happened now?" Gran asked.

When Maddie told her, Gran tutted.

"Oh, Maddie, you could have left it to Ethan. Just this once."

With her head in her hands, Maddie groaned. "He wants me to stay out of it and I keep ignoring him. I'm so worried that the wedding will be a disaster and that I might be ruining it myself."

Laura sat beside her. "Ethan loves you and he knows that your sleuthing is a part of who you are. He's only mad because he's scared for your safety."

Wiping her eyes with the back of her hand, Maddie nodded. "I know you're right, but I hate to see him angry with me."

"Well, if you two are going to marry, you'd better get used to it, because I can't see either of you changing anytime soon," Suzy said firmly.

"That doesn't make me feel better."

"Sorry. I just say it how I see it. Maybe you could make a pact to tell each other what you're planning. That way there aren't any surprises."

The corners of Maddie's mouth tugged upward. "That may be your best suggestion ever."

Suzy grinned. "I surprise myself sometimes. What will you do next?"

"I'll invite Ethan to dinner and cook a wonderful meal. Then I'll tell him everything I found out and leave it up to him to pursue while I concentrate on the wedding."

"That sounds perfect." Gran smiled sweetly.

Maddie sure hoped it would be. Just as she hoped she could keep any promise made to stay out of things. Gran didn't appear to think so.

Chapter Twenty-Six

Initially hesitant when Maddie called to ask him to come for dinner, it took a little persuasion until Ethan relented.

Now they sat in the apartment kitchen in an unusually awkward silence. Maddie couldn't bear it. "I'm sorry about not staying out of the case."

Ethan slowly put his knife and fork down. "Are you sorry, or sorry that you had to send Suzy for help?"

She gulped. "I won't lie to you. I knew you'd be upset, but I didn't think about it in the moment. When I walked into the bakery and found the doors open and my trial wedding cake ruined, it was too much."

"I didn't know that and I'm sorry, but it was just a cake." He ran fingers through his hair, and she ached at his frustration. "We've discussed this so many times. You're more important than anything else. I just don't know what to say to make you stop and think about the danger you place yourself in."

She put a hand over his. "Of course you're right about the cake and I know how hard it is for you to understand why I do what I do. When the clues start swirling in my head and I get a sense of them falling into place, I can't ignore them."

His mouth tightened. "More likely 'won't' ignore them."

"It's hard to fight it. Almost impossible. You know I try."

"You could try harder."

"I promise you that I have. Then thoughts eat away at me until I have to do something."

He shrugged. "It feels like we're at an impasse."

"Which scares me more than anything. I can't sleep because of it, but I don't think I can change." Maddie took a deep breath and admitted her deepest fear. The one that had been troubling her for months. "How can we get married and live together knowing there's this block that could tear us apart?"

His eyes widened. "Do you want to call it off?"

She leaned across the table and took one of his hands. "I want to be your wife more than anything. What I'm saying is that you have to accept me, warts and all."

He returned the pressure. "And I want to marry you, but this sounds very one-sided—I have to accept everything you do and say, no matter how I feel about it?"

She tilted her head. "I accept who you are and what you do."

"It's not the same. As a sheriff, it's my job to find the bad guys and solve the crimes. You're a baker. That should be a safe profession if you stay out of my cases."

"Your job puts you in danger. I don't like that at all, but I know that's not only your job but it's also a part of who you are. You want to help people. So do I, and I think I have a few skills which back that up to some extent."

He sat back. "So, what do we do about it?"

"If we intend to take our vows seriously, then we love

each other despite everything that frustrates and annoys us."

Ethan was silent for several heartbeats, but his eyes never left her face. "It's all or nothing with you—that's the deal?"

She nodded. "Can you handle that?"

"Do I have a choice?" He sighed again. "No need to answer. There is no choice for me. I love you. I want to marry you, but you can't expect me to embrace the amateur sleuth side of your personality the way I do the rest of you. I will always worry and more so when you're digging into things that you shouldn't."

"As long as you can love me when I do, I can live with that."

"How kind of you," he said wryly.

She looked at him hopefully. "So we're good?"

"As good as we can be." He shrugged. "When I look at the world, I guess ours is a darn sight better than it is for a lot of other couples."

Maddie winced, thinking about Laura and Rob, and felt the pressure of his fingers over hers.

"Just one thing, Maddie."

"What's that?"

"Do not expect me to reveal anything about a case."

"I won't expect it."

He shook a finger at her. "I know exactly what you mean and there is no wriggle room."

"No pillow talk?"

"None. Not ever."

She raised an eyebrow. "Are you sure about that?"

His mouth twitched. "You're incorrigible."

"And you are the handsomest and kindest and most understanding fiancé in the entire world."

167

This made him snort. "Yeah, flattery isn't going to work."

Maddie smiled, then took both his hands. "Look, I know we're joking about it, even though you're serious about everything you've said, and I want you to know that I am going to do my best not to scare you."

"But?" he drawled.

Her fingers twitched in his and she knew they would be doing a tap dance on her thighs if he let them go. He didn't, and she had to continue with them imprisoned. "I've been dying to talk to you about the case and to tell you what I think."

He grimaced. "Let's not use that particular phrase."

"Sorry. If you're done, can I show you my lists?"

Ethan pushed his plate away. "You may as well."

Maddie jumped up to grab her notebook off the counter and handed it to him. "These are all the details I wrote down after I got home from the bar and some more that I've added since."

Ethan took his time reading the two pages. "This is pretty concise."

"Thanks. It sounded to me like most people liked Buddy. Did you catch up with the ex-wife?"

He considered this briefly and must have concluded it was safe information. "We did. Nothing unusual there and she pretty much repeated what Laura told me about their relationship."

"And you went back to speak to Hugo?"

He shook his head. "I did go back to Destiny with that intention, but it looks like he left town."

"That can't be right." Maddie was genuinely surprised. "I only spoke to him a couple of times, but I got the impression that Hugo loved his job, and he certainly didn't mention anything about moving on."

"Perhaps it was a spur-of-the-moment thing," Ethan suggested, though he now seemed unsure.

Maddie's stomach twisted. "I have a bad feeling about this. Are you trying to track him down?"

Ethan nodded. "We are, but I'll escalate it further tomorrow."

Pleased, Maddie raised an eyebrow. "So I can be of use?"

"You do have some talents," he admitted. "However, if you sit there gloating, I'm not staying for dessert."

"How do you know there's dessert?"

"There's always dessert when you're trying to win me over."

She laughed. "Okay, no gloating, but I have to ask how the killer got the car inside the paddock without being seen or heard?"

He leaned back with his hands behind his head. "They didn't."

Sensing some smugness, she plowed ahead. "Angel and I saw tire tracks."

"You did see tracks, but they weren't from a car. The farmer who leases the fields from Gran had brought in a quad bike. He's getting older and it makes getting around his herd and the paddocks easier. Driving around the edge of the field beyond the one nearest to the road, he came through the gate separating them. When he ran out of gas, he left it where it was overnight."

Maddie blinked as it sunk in. "I didn't know about the quad bike."

"Which ironically points to me knowing how to do my

job. Still, I dare say you would have figured it out eventually," he said kindlier than she probably deserved.

She smiled, happy that the tension had evaporated as they talked. There was still the issue of Hugo's disappearance as well as the stranger in her kitchen, but it was time to give them a back seat. Ethan was more important, and he needed time out from worrying about her.

Plus, tomorrow was an exciting day.

Chapter Twenty-Seven

The dress was only the second one she'd tried on, but instantly Maddie had known it was the one when she and Angel had found it some weeks ago. The bodice fit like a glove and then dropped in shimmering fabric from her hips. As soon as she emerged from the fitting room, the Girlz and Gran buzzed around Maddie like moths to a flame.

Gran's eyes glistened. "It's gorgeous, sweetheart."

Laura clasped her hands to her chest. "You look like a princess."

"Wow!" Angel flapped her hands at her own face. "It's even more beautiful than I remembered. Ethan's gonna fall in love with you all over again."

"That's for sure." Suzy dabbed at the corners of her eyes. "Well, that's another tick off your list."

Biting back a small sob, Maddie twirled. The bottom of the dress floated out and then settled against her legs. "Thank goodness we found it so quickly, and I'm so glad you love it the way I do."

"What's not to love, sugar? It's like it was made for you."

She nodded. "I can't believe it's only one more week until I'm Mrs. Tanner."

"You're taking his name?" Suzy asked.

"Why wouldn't I?"

"Didn't you get the memo? It's not necessary these days."

"It might not be necessary, but I want to."

Angel glared at Suzy. "We each get to choose what works for us."

"Except for bridesmaid dresses." Maddie winked and pointed behind her. "They're waiting for you in the fitting room."

"Better not be some pink fluffy thing," Suzy muttered.

"You'll have to wait and see. Now shoo!" Gran scolded.

Twirling again and admiring her reflection, Maddie felt odd to be dressed this way. She eyed Gran and the changing rooms nervously. "I hope this works out okay. Maybe we should have checked before we picked the dresses."

"Too bad if they don't like them." Gran shrugged. "You do, and you're the one paying the bill."

Thankfully, it wasn't too long before her friends emerged from behind the curtains wearing the shimmering sheaths she and Gran picked with the help of the store owner.

Angel clapped her hands. "Good choice, sugar. Green is the perfect color for all of us."

"Even redheads?" Laura asked skeptically.

"That's an old fallacy," Angel assured her. "Trust me, it suits you the most."

"You're all stunning." Gran dabbed her eyes. "No one will be able to look away from my gorgeous Girlz."

They shared a group hug and after one last twirl, Maddie checked the clock on the wall. "Thankfully, I don't think any of them need altering, and we better get going if I'm to be on time for my meeting with Lyra at the community center."

"I wish we could be there to meet her." Suzy screwed up her nose. "But some of us have work to do."

"I'll be sure to introduce you at the wedding, and thanks for making time today."

"As if we wouldn't," Angel scoffed.

They hurried to the fitting rooms to change before Maddie signed the paperwork and made the final payment. Thankfully, Camille was the same size as Laura. Manhattan was a bit far to come for a fitting.

After dropping off the Girlz, Maddie and Gran hurried to the community center. A minute later, Lyra and her assistant pulled up outside just as Gran was unlocking the front door.

The chef didn't hesitate to hug Maddie and then she did the same to Gran. "It's so lovely to see you both again."

"I can't believe you're doing this for me, and I know the community center isn't what you're used to," Maddie began, suddenly nervous that Lyra would take one look inside and back out. Or would that happen when Maddie told her what had been happening in Maple Falls lately?

The celebrity chef took her arm. "Don't be silly. A wedding reception is all about the people, and you and your fiancé in particular make it special."

Maddie gave a weak smile. "That's how I feel about it and I promise it will look better on the day."

"I'm only the chef," Lyra told her firmly. "Everything else is none of my business."

"At least I know the food will be awesome."

Lyra stilled and stared into Maddie's eyes. "Why do I get the impression that something's wrong? You're not getting cold feet, are you?"

"Nothing like that." Maddie hiccupped. While not really wanting to talk about Buddy today, she understood that Lyra needed to know everything for her own satisfaction as well as safety, just as Maddie would. She had to be honest. "The thing is our wedding singer was found dead a while ago. He was murdered."

Lyra's fingers tightened on Maddie's arm. "Good grief. How are you even functioning?"

The kindness and lack of judgement was overwhelming, and Maddie almost lost it. They were alike in many ways, including not relishing the spotlight. Being the bride for a day was more than enough exposure for her, and the murder of Buddy had definitely gotten tongues wagging. Once it got out about Lyra being in town, interest would likely escalate.

She took a deep breath. "I keep telling myself the murder was nothing to do with the wedding, but a few days ago, someone went into my bakery and deliberately opened the oven door so my practice wedding cake would be ruined. I'd understand if you want to pull out."

Lyra's eyes widened. "I appreciate you telling me. It sounds like a warning."

"That's what I thought, but I can't see any connection to me."

"Except your fiancé happens to be the sheriff, right?"

Maddie gaped. "Oh. Of course. You think this is to scare Ethan into not investigating the murder?"

"Possibly."

"Ethan is a dedicated sheriff. He would never do that,

not even for me. But I guess someone who doesn't know him couldn't appreciate that. Anyway, I'm sorry about all this drama, and like I said, I would understand if you wanted to change your mind."

Lyra hadn't let go of her arm and now she took the other one. "You didn't walk away from my competition in Cozy Hollow when you knew there was an issue. In fact, you pitched in to help. This is my chance to return the favor."

For the first time, Maggie Parker, Lyra's assistant and good friend, spoke up. "In that case, Dan will be coming to keep an eye on you."

Lyra gave a wry smile at the no-nonsense statement. "We'd be hard-pressed to keep your fiancé away once he hears about this and it won't hurt to have an extra pair of eyes on proceedings."

For a moment, Maddie was stunned. Daniel Best had been head of Lyra's security and her driver. Ex-army, he was now a mechanic, but he was always available whenever Lyra needed him. "I can't thank you enough, and I'm sure Ethan will be delighted to know Dan is on hand. One of his deputies is supposed to be our best man and Detective Jones is also in the wedding party."

Lyra dropped her arms. "Excellent. That means we should all be safe enough. Now that's all settled, let's check out the kitchen so I know what I have to work with. Then you can tell me all about how you want the food to look and the timings."

The next hour was fun for the four women as they discussed everything from the plates to be used and the plating of each dish. While Maddie and Lyra had worked out the menu, Maddie would have no hand in the cooking. It was a big call not to interfere, but as far as Maddie was concerned, Lyra was the best in the business. It would be stupidity to interfere.

With her notebook on the counter and a great deal of satisfaction, they ticked off the last thing on her list.

The last thing except for Rob. Would Ethan have a best man?

Chapter Twenty-Eight

There was no time for a dress rehearsal, and Ethan didn't want a bachelor party, but at Gran's suggestion, Ethan had organized a supper at his place the week before the wedding for the bridesmaids and groomsmen.

Though it was very impromptu, Maddie agreed it was necessary. Not only was there an issue with Rob and Laura, but Ethan had picked Steve Jones as his best man. While they were hoping to foster a working relationship for the day with the first two, Steve's inclusion still puzzled her and Angel wasn't as delighted as she might be about it.

Slipping an arm around Ethan's waist, she peered up at him. "Is Steve coming tonight?"

Ethan let the last bottle of beer settle into the ice bucket he'd been filling. "He hopes to stop by for an hour."

"Hmm."

Ethan sighed. "That sounded ominous. What's bothering you?"

"Aside from the whole Buddy thing?"

He chuckled. "Yeah, besides that."

"Well, I don't want to sound rude, but why is Steve your best man?"

Ethan studied the bucket and bent to switch a couple of bottles to the top. "You know my best friends are out of the country and it was pretty short notice in the end."

Maddie felt a twinge of guilt at the way she'd dithered with venues. "I understand that, but there are so many people you've known longer to choose from."

"Like Rob? In the end, I decided it wasn't worth the drama. He's swallowed some of his pride and agreed to stand up with me, but I'd kick myself if he ruined our day. Plus, I thought it should be someone who won't be looking for favors in the future."

She smiled when he winked at her. "That makes a great deal of sense. I appreciate you have to keep your job separate."

He kissed her forehead. "It was a no-brainer really. We have more than enough going on, and despite his promises, who knows how Rob will be on the day."

"I guess we'll get a taste of it soon." Maddie nodded to the path. "Here comes Rob now, and Laura's in the kitchen mixing up a punch."

The deputy handed Ethan a bottle of wine and gave Maddie a sheepish glance. "Thanks for inviting me."

"We're pleased you came. Can I get you a drink?"

"I'll take a soda if you have any."

"Sure. There's plenty in the kitchen."

Ethan chuckled behind them as Maddie led Rob through the house. It was better to get this over with. Much like ripping off a Band-Aid.

Laura was stirring a large punch bowl and must have heard them as she looked over her shoulder. Eyes wide, she stared at Rob. Maddie sighed. It wasn't as though she didn't know Rob was coming tonight. In fact, Maddie had had to convince her to come.

"Rob would like a soda," Maddie explained.

Laura pointed to the counter. "There's some out, or you can help yourself from the refrigerator."

Not exactly a warm reception, but at least Laura had acknowledged him.

Rob grabbed a can. "This will do fine. Ah, I'm on call tonight, but I wanted to come and apologize for my behavior."

Maddie should have left. It would have been the right thing to do. Only, these two weren't known for having clear conversations, and this might be the only chance to get it all out in the open before the wedding.

Laura let the spoon slide into the bowl and turned slowly. "Thank you. I'm sorry I didn't tell you about having drinks with Buddy. It all happened so fast, and I do love music."

"Yes, you do," Rob replied agreeably.

Maddie helped herself to a soda and backed up to the doorway. Was it safe to leave or was Laura going to tell him about the kiss?

"I didn't like how you treated me," Laura told him. "You've always been kind, and I wasn't aware you had that kind of anger inside you."

Maddie wanted to cheer.

Rob paled. "I didn't know either. I saw you with him and it was like a red mist descended over me. I couldn't seem to get past you being so happy with someone else."

"You can be happy with more than one person."

He shrugged. "I hear that's true, but I've never felt about anyone the way I feel about you. And the way he was looking at you told me he wanted more than a drink."

Maddie felt someone beside her. It was Steve, and if he'd worn a hair shirt, he couldn't have looked more uncomfortable. She nodded for them to leave and Steve nodded back with a great deal of enthusiasm.

"That was awkward," he said once they were in the sitting room.

"Incredibly," she agreed. "I hope that the air will be cleared enough for them to be civil at the wedding."

"Don't you worry about Rob. I'll keep him in line if he doesn't behave himself."

Maddie couldn't help a chuckle at the look on Steve's face. "As long as you don't hurt him."

"What? Oh, you're teasing me. I promise there will be no altercation." He winked. "And you won't see the bruises."

This time she laughed outright. Steve wasn't known for his humor. "Thanks for stepping in as Best Man."

"Ethan did twist my arm, but I must admit the privilege is all mine. He's one of the good guys."

Maddie smiled, suddenly deciding that she liked him more than she thought. They'd known each other for some time, but he was always so cool and collected that she'd rarely glimpsed another side to him. And certainly not this humorous one. "I'm glad you think so, because I certainly do. And I'm glad he has you to stand beside him." She leaned in. "He says you're one of the good guys too."

"Well, he would. Seeing as how I'm kinda out rank him. And we do work well together."

They were both laughing when Angel walked in.

"A person could die waiting for a drink around here," she said pointedly.

Gorgeous as always, the sleeveless short sky-blue dress showed off her long tanned legs to perfection.

Steve was not immune. "We can't have that. What would you like?"

Angel winked. "Tell me what you've got, sugar."

Maddie made a quick exit. It was time to leave her friends to their confusing relationships and get back to her own. She found Ethan right where she'd left him, but now Gran was there with Luke and Suzy.

Luke took a beer from Ethan. "This is a great place."

"Yep, it sure is," Ethan said proudly.

Though Ethan smiled, Maddie understood he really would miss the house that had belonged to his parents and where he'd grown up. "We'll be back here one day," she promised.

He pulled her braid gently. "I know, and I swear I'll get my stuff to your place in the next couple of days."

"So you aren't selling?" Luke asked. "Who's going to live here?"

"No one."

"Would you consider renting it?"

Ethan shuddered. "Frankly, the thought of someone else living here gives me hives."

Luke looked away. "Oh. Fair enough. I might go see if I can find Beth."

"I guess he's keen to get out of home," Suzy noted.

Ethan frowned. "You mean he was asking for himself?"

"Yes!" the rest of them chorused.

"Okay, okay. I didn't get that. Still, I don't think it changes anything."

Maddie put her arm through his. "It's your house to rent or not rent."

"Only for one more week," he reminded her. "Then it's our house."

She smiled at the image his words evoked. They would

raise a family here one day. Just not right now. "Then I guess you'll own half a bakery."

He grimaced. "I hope that doesn't mean I have to learn to bake."

Suzy snorted. "Well, it would be fair, since Maddie does love to solve mysteries."

They all laughed at that, but Ethan was shaking his head. He couldn't possibly argue with the truth—and neither could she.

It was as if they'd put the frustration of the case not being resolved before the wedding aside for tonight, and they might have to for a few more days yet. That was going to be hard when the threads of the case constantly nagged at her to find a way to join them together.

Chapter Twenty-Nine

The week went by in a rush of excitement and nerves. With the bakery closed, Maddie had all day to get ready, yet staying in bed wasn't an option. Used to waking so early, and too excited to try to get back to sleep, she was up and dressed in sweatpants and a T-shirt.

Big Red had been especially smoochy as if he sensed this would be the last day it would be just the two of them. He wouldn't be too happy to have Ethan share her bed, but he'd have to get used to it.

There was a voice message to say Ethan couldn't wait to see her, which meant he hadn't slept much either. She hoped it was from excitement and nothing else and sent him a message about being patient just as Camille came out of the spare room in a similar ensemble.

Her friend had arrived last night, and they'd stayed up reminiscing and putting the ghost to bed over Camille's tragic loss so there would be no upset today—Maddie hoped.

Pushing hair from her face, Camille stretched and when

she spied Maddie on the sofa, raced across the room to hug her tightly. "Happy wedding day!"

Maddie's words came out in a rush. "I still can't quite believe it's happening."

"Well, you only have a couple of hours before the big moment, so you better believe it."

Big Red leapt from the chair and ran downstairs just as they heard the door open. This was followed by soft footfalls on the stairs.

"Are you up?" Gran whispered.

"We sure are. What are you doing here at this time of the day?"

Gran entered the room beaming. "I've come to make my granddaughter breakfast, and I have a surprise. Can you come downstairs?"

Maddie was grinning as she hurried down the stairs after Gran and then slid to a stop halfway across the kitchen. "Ava! Mom!"

Her mom had peeked out from behind the corner of the office, and she laughed. "I prefer Mom, but whatever."

Their strained relationship had eased considerably when Maddie and Gran went to England to visit Ava and her new husband in their run-down castle. Maddie was truly delighted to see her mom. "I thought you couldn't make it?"

"Your stepfather stayed behind to take care of things but insisted I come. Like he said, I only have one child, and I've missed so many of your special days. I'd been feeling rather devastated over missing out on seeing you get married, so in the end it was an easy decision."

Maddie sniffed. "Oh, Mom. You don't know how much it means to have you here."

Her mom opened her arms, and they hugged. This was

the relationship Maddie had always craved to have with her mom. The timing was perfect.

Gran sniffed, her arm around Camille. "Right, what does everyone want?"

"Blueberry pancakes!" Mother and daughter said together.

"On their way. Ava, would you make the tea?"

"Yes, Mom."

If Maddie's and Ava's relationship had been strained, it was far worse for Ava and Gran who had butted heads all their lives. The sight of them in her bakery enjoying each other's company like a real family made Maddie so happy, she could barely contain the tears that threatened again.

Gran whipped up the batter in no time and had just poured some onto the griddle when the door opened and Angel arrived in a yellow T-shirt and yoga pants.

"I knew it!"

"Don't tell me you could smell the food from your place?" Maddie's mom asked wryly.

"Not quite, but I had a feeling you'd all be awake, and I didn't want to miss a minute of today. My bestie is getting married and I'm so excited."

"Me too." Laura entered the kitchen, still a little shy around Ava, and gave Maddie a hug.

The last to arrive was Suzy. The pocket rocket was doing her best not to get emotional and was losing the battle as she sniffed her way through a stack of pancakes.

They'd just finished breakfast when a van and a car pulled up outside. It had made more sense to use Maddie's industrial kitchen to prepare and cook most of the food then move it to the community center to heat and serve.

"She's here. She's really here!" Maddie yelled like a kid at Christmas.

Angel sighed enviously as she stared out the window. "She's as gorgeous in real life as she looks on TV."

"This is so surreal. I love her." Laura hid behind Gran.

Maddie stood in the middle of the room tapping her thigh. "Don't be nervous. She's lovely and so down to earth."

"But it's Lyra St. Claire," Laura protested. "She's famous."

"Perhaps one of you could let her in?" her mom suggested, eyeing Maddie's fingers drumming on her thigh. No one moved, and in the end, Ava opened the door herself.

"Good morning. I'm Ava, Maddie's mom."

"Pleased to meet you, and it's not hard to see the likeness. I'm Lyra."

Maddie's mom laughed. "I'm pretty sure there isn't a person in a thousand miles who doesn't know who you are, dear. Come in and make yourself at home. There are plenty of pancakes for you and your team if you're hungry after the drive. Just tell us what you need, then we'll get out of your hair."

Lyra smiled and swept into the kitchen. "A straight talker like your daughter. I like that." She came to Maddie and gave her a hug. "How are you doing?"

"I'm so happy and excited I could burst."

"Well, don't do that. I can see your kitchen is sparkling clean, so show me around and then we'll check the menu one last time to settle your nerves while my staff brings everything in. After that, you can leave this part of things to us."

Maddie nodded and felt a small knot unwind in her mind. Then she greeted Maggie and Dan as they helped bring in what Lyra had brought with her. They pored over the menu for several minutes without the need for explanations. It was simple, but with Lyra's flair, it would be amazing. Maddie was looking forward to tasting everything.

There was something about watching the precision of Lyra's team as they unpacked that soothed Maddie, and she knew she didn't have to worry.

"Where's the cake?"

Maddie pointed to her desk where three boxes sat side by side. "It's all packaged up and ready to go." Knowing that the layers were as perfect as she could make them and so happy with how the honey cake turned out, there was a fair measure of pride in her voice.

Gran pushed her gently. "Then I think you're done here. I'll clean up the breakfast things and make sure Lyra has everything she needs. Get upstairs and enjoy your time with the Girlz."

Maddie smiled gratefully. Everything she wanted was organized and planned. Now she must trust her family and friends to deliver. While it was one of the hardest things she had ever asked of herself, it was time to let go.

And hope that the killer would leave them be.

Chapter Thirty

By the time they were ready and came back downstairs, the kitchen smelled heavenly. Lyra and Maggie grinned and gave her a thumbs-up as they walked by.

Luke drove Honey, who had been polished for the occasion and was decorated by the Girlz. Now they waited in the vestibule of the church. Maddie's heart pounded as Gran, eyes shining with love and unshed tears, smoothed the flowing white dress that nipped in at Maddie's waist.

Gran straightened the small veil, which sat on her long blonde hair, released for a change from its braid, and wrapped her arm through Maddie's. "I know being the center of attention is difficult for you, but try to enjoy each moment, sweetheart. The memories will be worth it."

Maddie smiled, swallowing the lump in her throat. Gran and Grandad had loved each other deeply, and while her mom hadn't had any success in relationships until recently, her grandparents stood out as a beacon for what love should look like.

Burying her nose for an instant in the fragrant bundle she held, Maddie smiled. Of course it held myrtle. Every royal bride since Queen Victoria carried myrtle, and since it symbolized love and hope, Gran, a devoted anglophile, had whole heartedly approved. There was also baby's breath or gypsophila, tiny pink roses, and yellow tulips.

Lifting her chin, she nodded at the women in front of her. "Let's go, Girlz."

Gran signaled to Luke, who opened the doors. First to walk through were the twins, James and Jessie Dixon, Ethan's nephews. The lovable rascals had already been given a stern talking to by their mom, Layla, who hovered nearby as they walked sedately down the aisle. Next were her bridesmaids led by Angel. Along with Suzy, Camille, and then Laura, just as Gran had said, they were gorgeous in their green shifts. With a deep breath, Maddie and Gran moved forward, still clutching each other's arm.

The church held more flowers than a florist's shop and Mavis grinned from the second pew. Making an effort to smile at the guests, Maddie's gaze was drawn to the altar where Ethan stood by the minister. She knew Rob was beside him as well as Steve Jones and Luke, but her focus was on the man she had loved for most of her life.

Ethan, so handsome in his tuxedo, grinned at her and the room melted away. When he held out his hand, Maddie all but floated to his side. Gran snuck in a brief hug before letting her go. Then Angel tapped her shoulder, and Maddie handed her the bouquet.

Her bridesmaids lined up beside Angel. The Girlz and Camille beamed at her and she smiled back. Gran had taken her seat next to Ava in the front pew. Seeing them together, Maddie thought her heart would burst. Turning back to Ethan, her mouth quivered. Seeing his concern, she smiled. "I'm happy crying," she whispered.

Unfortunately, the microphone near the minister was on and the words echoed through the church. There was a moment's silence and then she heard her mom snort, followed by the Girlz. Maddie shrugged. "You'll get used to it."

Another round of laughter stalled when Ethan kissed her hand. "That's the only crying I wish for you for the rest of our lives. Before we say our vows, I have something to say."

Maddie gulped.

"From the moment I saw you upside down on the jungle gym with that braid of yours dangling on the ground and then swinging fearlessly from the monkey bars, I was smitten. You have always been clever, talented, kind, and so determined that I got scared you would find me not enough. I was young and stupid and put you through some tough times. With my job, I still do. There's not much I can do about that, but I promise to be careful, honest, and faithful. I'll protect you while trying not to be overprotective." He paused for the laughter that he obviously knew would follow. "I'll listen, even when I don't want to hear certain things. And I will love you with all that I am, no matter what."

Ethan wasn't normally so open about his feelings, especially not in such a group situation, so Maddie was lost for a minute and needed time to get her emotions under control. When she thought she could speak, she licked her lips and swallowed hard.

"Whether I wanted it or not, you have protected me from so much. When Grandad passed, you were there for me, and you helped me say goodbye. I realize in this moment just how much I depended on you when we were growing up and it wasn't always fair. Not when I knew what you wanted and that I wasn't ready. I should have explained my feelings on that a lot better." She looked briefly at her mom and smiled. "But we can't change the past, and I have no regrets, because here we are at the right time and in the right place, surrounded by people we love, who love us. There was never anyone else who could fill the space in my heart the way that you do and there never will be. I choose you, Ethan, and I will love you forever, no matter what."

They were both tearful as the minister got them to say their traditional vows and though she heard the sniffles behind her from the guests, Maddie managed to mute them so it felt like it was just the two of them speaking to each other. The twins solemnly held out the cushions with the matching wedding bands and soon after came the beautiful words she had waited for.

"You may kiss your bride."

Ethan pulled her to him as if he had been desperate for this moment. As she melted into his arms, whistles and cheers rang out and brought her back to where they were. Both pink-cheeked, they turned to face their friends and families before walking down the aisle as husband and wife.

Maddie let that sink in. She was a wife now and married to the man she had always loved. It was almost overwhelming, and as if he sensed it, Ethan squeezed her hand and moved a little closer. Maddie wiped the corner of her eyes. The moment was perfect, and she would never forget this feeling of everything being right with her world. Whatever the future held, they had each other, and this was no time for tears—even if they were happy ones.

Outside, Angel was the first to congratulate and kiss them, followed by Gran and the Girlz, and then it was a free-for-all, which passed in a blur of well-wishers, hugs, and more kisses.

Luke waited outside in front of the church with Honey's doors open and Ethan settled Maddie inside.

"Take us for a ride somewhere quiet for five minutes," he instructed.

Luke grinned. "You bet."

He drove them up to the lookout at the top of the hill leading to Destiny.

Ethan helped her out and they walked to the seat that perched there. Taking off his jacket, he put it on the worn wooden slats so she could sit without marking her dress. When he sat beside her, Ethan turned and took her face in his palms before he kissed her.

"Hello, Mrs. Tanner."

"Hello, Mr. Tanner. That was a lovely speech you gave."

"Considering I left my notes at my house, it wasn't too bad. More importantly, I meant every word."

"Me too. It was perfect and thanks for bringing me up here to catch our breath. It was a bit much, wasn't it?"

He snorted. "And it's not over yet. Considering what we do for jobs, you'd think a wedding would be a piece of cake."

"True. Neither of us like a fuss and yet we're always in the middle of one. At least, that's how it seems."

He shrugged. "I guess life is never boring."

"You can say that again. Now, as nice as this is and I appreciate why we're here, we should get back to our guests. There are photos to take."

Ethan grimaced. "Then you'd better kiss me again so I

have something else to think about while we are forced to make small talk."

That kiss made it even more difficult to leave, but people were waiting.

Chapter Thirty-One

As previously organized, they met the rest of the bridal party on the green for photos. Thirty minutes later, they were walking into the community center, which looked vastly different. Trees of balloons and white walls dripping with lights as well as more flowers greeted them along with the guests.

Noah paused the soft music. "Please raise your glasses to Mr. and Mrs. Tanner."

"To Mr. and Mrs. Tanner!" the guests chorused.

After another few moments, Noah spoke again. "If you would all kindly take your seats, the proceedings are about to begin."

While they slowly did as asked, Maddie snuck into the kitchen and found Lyra issuing orders for the entree. "Is everything okay?"

Rosy-cheeked from cooking, Lyra laughed. "I suspected you'd come to check on things. While I don't mind, this is your wedding. Everything is going to plan, so I don't want to see you again until we're done."

"Are you sure I can't...?"

"I'm positive." Lyra waved her away. "Now, get out of here before I call for your gran."

"How could I doubt your talent or the threat?" Maddie took one last look and gave a slight bow, only to find her husband waiting at the door, an eyebrow raised.

"Couldn't help yourself?"

She laughed. "It's the nature of this beast."

"And are you happy with everything?"

"I am. Lyra is a star in every way. Shall we get this party started?"

He held out his arm and they took their seats at the bridal table.

From that moment, everything ran like a well-oiled machine, and though Maddie had no written list, she could see it in her head—each item had a resounding tick beside it. The food was excellent as expected, the speeches were funny and touching. Eventually, and at just the right moment, Lyra wheeled out the cake. Maddie saw her give the cake one final check and then place a knife beside it. After that, she hurried back into the kitchen before too many people saw her.

There were a few nods and whispers, but before anyone got too carried away with a celebrity in their midst, Noah called their attention to the cutting of the cake and the moment passed.

Together, hand over hand, Ethan and Maddie sliced through the layer of soft honey cake and pulled out a large triangle. They broke some off and fed each other a piece.

"Thank goodness. It's perfect," she whispered.

Ethan grinned. "Just like you."

"And now for the first dance," Noah announced.

Her new husband's grin disappeared. "Ah, my worst nightmare. I wish we'd had time to practice."

She laughed. "Just sway a little and we'll be fine," Maddie assured him as she slipped into his arms.

They circled the floor once before she sent a pointed look to the Girlz.

Angel poked out her tongue but sashayed up to the detective and took his arm. The poor man looked scared, which was so out of character. To his credit, Steve straightened his shoulders as if going into battle and followed her to the dance floor. Laura's face paled and she sidled up to Luke, who shrugged and took her hand. Finally, Suzy, whose face was as dark as thunder, pointed to Rob and then to the dancers. His head bowed but Rob allowed her to lead him to the edge of the floor. Camille put her hands out to the twins who were overly enthusiastic.

"Oh dear, I feel like we might be asking too much of our attendants." Maddie chuckled into Ethan's ear.

"Hah! Too bad. It's not our fault they're all cowards."

Maddie laughed. "I hope you're talking about the men."

"Mostly. Camille deserves a medal for bravery, but Steve's like a clam when it comes to feelings, and Rob's got a ton of guilt on his shoulders. Frankly, they look scared of women."

Ethan had enjoyed a couple of glasses of champagne and was as relaxed as she'd ever seen him.

"Unlike you?" she teased.

His gaze slid over her. "Oh, I'd be a fool not to be a little scared, but more of a fool not to take a chance."

Maddie tilted her head. Considering the women and men in their lives, this was definitely food for thought. For different reasons, the Girlz were nervous about any relationship, and so were the men. While she didn't want to be a matchmaker, it would be wonderful if they could all find

197

love, but how could they when they were so scared of making a mistake?

"I can hear you thinking." Ethan interrupted her reverie.

She tilted her head back so she could look at him. "So you keep saying. How is that possible?"

"Your body hums and you make little noises."

She blinked, considered if that were true and decided it probably was. "Grandad would be disappointed that I had a tell."

"I doubt he would ever be disappointed in you."

She smiled. They'd certainly had a special bond and Grandad told her straight up if he didn't like something, but he never put her down. Maybe that's why she loved Ethan. The two men were very much alike.

Leaning into this day had been great advice and she could see that Ethan was enjoying it almost as much as she was. There wasn't anything she could have done to make it better. Not even having it at the resort. In that scenario, there was no Lyra St. Claire, and her friend had certainly taken a massive weight off her shoulders by doing the catering. No, this day was perfect just the way it was—

A scream rent the air and Maddie's blood ran cold.

Not here.

Not today.

Chapter Thirty-Two

Out in the courtyard, Beth bent over a still form. Her hands were covered in blood as she applied pressure to a wound. "Help! Please someone help him!"

Having pushed their way through the crowd to get there first, Maddie let out an agonized groan and, heedless of her beautiful dress, dropped to her knees beside Beth.

"Who is it?" Mavis called.

"It's Luke," Ethan growled as his eyes scanned the crowd, searching for the perpetrator.

"Luke?" Nora gasped. "Maddie's baker and the friend of that Buddy guy who got killed?"

"Okay, everybody, move back," Ethan bellowed. "Now!"

Maddie ignored him and checking for a pulse, her words came out in a rush. "He's alive! We need an ambulance right away. Somebody get the first aid kit from the kitchen and cloths to stem this bleeding. We need a blanket too."

Someone thrust a shawl at Maddie and she handed it to

Beth. "Press it to the wound as hard as you can. We need to stop the blood."

Eyes wide, the young woman took it and did as she was asked without a murmur, though her mouth quivered, and tears rolled silently down her pale cheeks.

There was a lot of whispering and shuffling from behind until Ethan's gruff voice asked them to move. He crouched beside them and opened up the first aid kit that Lyra handed him. Pulling out a wad of packing, he gently removed Beth's hands and then the bloodied shawl. Gathering a handful of white shirt from each side, he yanked hard, and buttons flung in all directions. A couple pinged off two overturned glasses nearby. After taking a quick look, Ethan placed the wadding on the wound and pressed down hard.

To Maddie it looked like a knife wound and it looked deep. She took an edge of the shawl and wiped Beth's hands. The young woman's eyes never left Luke's face, and she didn't seem to be aware of Maddie's ministrations.

"Would you step over here, miss?" Steve Jones asked Beth, making the request sound more like a command.

Maddie squeezed Beth's hands and eventually she looked up. "The detective needs to talk to you."

Hesitant, and with jerky movements, Beth eventually complied without argument. This alone spoke of her shock and how upset she was. Rob brought a chair for her and when she was seated, the detective ushered everyone else back into the community center and closed the french doors.

Ethan placed a hand on Maddie's shoulder and squeezed. "You should go inside too."

Maddie shook her head and clutched Luke's cold hand. "I'm not leaving him."

He didn't ask again, but they looked hopelessly at each other while they waited for the ambulance. Weddings weren't supposed to end this way.

When the paramedics arrived and patched Luke up enough to travel, Beth insisted she should go with Luke, but Steve pressed her back into the chair. "I'm afraid you can't. As far as we are aware, you're the only witness and I need to ask you a few questions."

"I'll go with him." Maddie squeezed one of Beth's cold hands. "You know I'll make sure he has the best care."

The young woman blinked and after a moment, she nodded. "I trust you."

The way she said it made Maddie pause, but the paramedics were already lifting Luke onto the gurney. Since Angel had led them around the back, this meant they didn't need to go through the community center, which Maddie was grateful for.

Ethan wiped his hands on a cloth and followed them to the ambulance. "Are you sure about this?"

She turned to face him. "You mean about leaving the wedding?"

He nodded.

Placing a hand on his cheek, she gave a watery smile. "We both know that after this, the wedding is over. I'm okay with going with Luke because we did get married, and it was a wonderful day until this." Maddie waved a hand at the paramedics lifting Luke into the ambulance. "He needs me, and you don't right now. Are you okay with that?"

He nodded again, though he clearly as disappointed as she was with how the day was ending. "See you soon—I hope."

After a quick peck on her cheek, Ethan moved away, and she waved to him out the back of the ambulance as it drove away. He stayed there until they turned a corner, and she pictured him switching into sheriff mode. While he didn't have quite the same attachment to Luke as she did, he truly cared and thought highly of him, as evidenced by including him in the wedding party. Maddie was convinced that Ethan would leave no stone unturned to find out who did this terrible thing.

Angry tears ran down her cheeks as it sank in that Luke could die. The worst part about this, apart from Luke being attacked, was that she had known it wasn't over. She'd even suspected the wedding would be affected. Why hadn't she listened to herself?

Sirens blaring, it was the fastest trip to Destiny she'd ever experienced. After they were taken to the emergency department, Maddie was shown to the waiting room while they attended to Luke.

It was a busy place as usual and in her wedding dress, she stood out like a sore thumb. Naturally, people stared at the bride with blood on her dress. She went to the bathroom to wash her hands and tried to get rid of the bloodstains, but to no avail.

Back in the waiting room, with no bag and no phone, she was left to her thoughts, which centered around the crime. *Crimes*, she reminded herself.

Everything had to be connected, but how? Why had the killer attacked Luke? He was no threat to anyone. Unless he knew something. Or had seen something. Though she had asked him several times, he'd always denied that Buddy had any enemies. Only, what if he wasn't aware of the importance of anything he had seen—because he didn't really know Buddy as well as he wanted to think?

What could that look like to Luke? Sitting in a bar where people were drinking heavily and he wasn't, a fight would stand out. As would a strong argument. If there was none of that, then it had to be done in secret, because something had happened to spur the killer to take action. What might set a person off to do something so awful? Drink or drugs could have fueled it but what if it was more about jealousy?

Maddie plucked at the shiny pattern on her dress. Hugo made it sound like Buddy's friend had been usurped by Luke. Granted, killing Buddy because of it was extreme, and to then kill Luke seemed backward. If he had killed Luke first, which was an awful thought, then he wouldn't have had to kill Buddy.

The dark thoughts made her shiver, though jealousy didn't seem enough. Then she heard familiar and welcome voices. The door of the waiting room slid open to admit the Girlz as well as Gran, Ava, and Camille.

Angel knelt in front of her. "How are you doing, sugar?"

Maddie shrugged and leaned into the hug from Gran. "I'm okay." The truth was she had felt alone and upset about Luke as well as the wedding ending the way it had.

"No, you're not," Angel said as if reading her mind. "That's why we're here. So you're not alone."

"Any news on Luke?" Laura asked through stifled sobs.

"Nothing yet."

"I hope it's soon. She hasn't stopped crying," Suzy noted.

Her mom kissed Maddie's forehead and handed her a bag. "Sorry we've been so long. We made the detective talk to us first, then stopped off and got changed and packed you something else to wear."

"Thanks, Mom. I didn't expect everyone, but I'm glad you're all here. Is Ethan all right?"

"He's well into sheriff mode, which is kinda weird with

him wearing a tux." Camille plucked little clips from her hair. "They'll be there a while with all the interviewing they have to do."

"I'm so sorry, Camille. This must be dragging up bad memories for you."

Camille patted her arm. "It's sweet of you to worry about me and I admit it was a shock. If there is a good side to this, it's that you'd had the best of the day. That's all I wanted for you. Hopefully, once Luke recovers and this case is solved, you can forget what happened after."

Laura shuddered. "If he recovers."

Gran stood and nodded to her daughter to take her seat, then she pulled Laura to the corner of the room. "That kind of talk won't help him and only upsets everyone else. I know you feel responsible, but that's utter garbage, which deep down you know. Stop tormenting yourself, right this minute."

The room wasn't so large that they couldn't hear every word though everyone tried to pretend they hadn't. Gran didn't often use that tone and though it was said with love, it was firm. If Laura was wise, she would heed Gran's words.

Not knowing how long they had to wait, Maddie excused herself and went to the restroom to change. Catching sight of her tear-stained cheeks in the mirror, she gave her face a quick wash and used her fingers to rub the mascara from under her eyes. At least she could take off the shoes that pinched her toes and replace them with comfy sneakers—her usual footwear. The track pants and sweat-shirt were more comfortable, too, and once she removed her phone from the bottom of the now-empty bag, she barely took two seconds to stuff the dress into it.

The wedding was over and there was no point brooding over it. Her focus had to be on Luke—and solving the crimes. After marching back to where the others waited, she paced the room. Gran and Laura had returned to the fold, and it was a relief to see that Laura had stopped crying, even if her lips still quivered.

"I know they were only getting started with the questioning when you all left, but did anyone mention seeing anything odd before Luke was attacked?"

The group looked at each other and shook their heads.

"Not that we heard, and I can't say I hung around to listen to all the conjecture that was being bandied about," Gran told her.

"Why do you think Luke was out on the patio?" Maddie asked the most important question.

Laura took a shuddering breath. "He was talking to Beth."

Maddie nodded. "When Ethan and I got there, we found her pressing on the wound. She was distraught. When I think about it, there wasn't much blood around the area, just underneath him."

Angel gasped. "You can't think Beth stabbed him?"

"No, I don't. Only, she must have seen who did it."

"Not necessarily." Gran pursed her lips. "I saw Luke at the bar fetching two drinks when I came out of the restroom. Beth was in there putting on lip gloss."

"You think he was taking the drinks to Beth?"

"Probably, but that's not a given."

Maddie's skin prickled. "He would have gotten outside before Beth and it's more than likely that the killer was waiting for him, but it would have happened fast if Beth was on her way."

Her mom put a hand on her arm. "Sit down. You're getting worked up and I understand why, but you can't do a thing from here. You have one job right now and it isn't solving this crime. You must be here for Luke when he needs you."

Her mom was right, but that didn't stop Maddie from willing Ethan to phone her. With time on her hands, she phoned Lyra to apologize profusely, make sure she and her team were okay and to thank her for making the day so special.

Lyra tutted. "You're so sweet to give me a thought right now. Everything is fine and the guests have gone. We've nearly done with the clean up, so don't spare that a thought either. I'm just glad you got to enjoy most of your day and I'm sorry this happened to mar it."

Maddie swallowed hard. "You're so kind. I won't forget all that you've done when my time comes to help you."

"I know you won't. Now go be with your friends and don't worry about what's happening here. I wish Luke all the best. He seems like a lovely young man."

"He is. Thanks again, Lyra." Maddie bit back a sob and ended the call just in time.

Chapter Thirty-Three

Twenty minutes later, Ethan still hadn't phoned, though Rob did. He wanted to know how Luke was. Once she'd said there was no update yet, Maddie attempted to get any information she could. Unfortunately, Rob wasn't saying a word, and he ended the call abruptly just as a doctor came into the room.

Eyeing the large group warily as they swarmed around him, the doctor was all business. "You're all here for Mr. Luke Chisholm?"

Maddie nodded. "Is he going to be okay?"

"He is one very lucky young man. The blade missed all his organs. Stopping the bleeding as soon as you did saved his life."

A collective sigh of relief ran around the room.

"That was Beth. Thank goodness she acted quickly. Will he recover okay?" Maddie asked, still worried for her friend and riddled with guilt it had happened at all.

"I can't see any reason why he won't. Obviously, he'll need to take it easy while the wound heals, but the blood transfusion is helping, and he'll likely be discharged before the night's out."

"Really. Do you think that wise?" Laura blushed when the doctor frowned. "I mean, if the wound was quite deep, wouldn't he be better off here under proper care?"

He shook his head. "I believe he lives with his parents, so as long as he doesn't lift anything heavy or do anything too strenuous for a few days, he'll be fine."

"His parents are away," Maddie intervened.

The doctor frowned again. "Mr. Chisholm gave me the impression his parents would be available to care for him."

"Luke might have misunderstood you." Maddie had the sneaking suspicion Luke simply didn't want to bother anyone, or perhaps he just wanted out of the hospital. "Either way, we'll make sure he's not alone. May we see him?"

"He's had painkillers, so he's a bit woozy and shouldn't be exposed to any excitement, but if the police say it's okay, one of you can come see him for a few minutes once they're done with him."

It made sense that the police would be here after an attempted murder, but would they let Maddie see him? "Do you know which deputy is here?"

The doctor checked his notes. "Actually, it's Detective Jones."

She nodded, a little apprehensive about having to deal with Steve at some stage tonight, but at least Luke would be safe with the detective here. "Thank you, Doctor. We'll wait to hear."

Now it was back to waiting. Camille and Laura fetched coffee and tea for everyone. Suzy messaged her parents who were on holiday, while Ava and Angel flicked through ancient magazines, but Maddie couldn't settle. It was another half hour before a nurse came out and glanced around the group.

"Maddie Flynn?"

She scrambled to her feet. "That's me."

"You can see Mr. Chisholm for a few minutes. I'll take you through."

Maddie glanced at the others.

"You go," Gran told her. "Take as long as you need."

Nodding gratefully, Maddie followed the nurse to the room where Luke lay as white as the sheets. The drip in his arm held a white fluid and when she took the seat beside the bed, his eyes flickered open.

"Hey, Maddie," he croaked.

"Hey, there. I'm so glad you're okay. How do you feel?"

His eyes filled with sorrow. "Pathetically weak and so sorry that I didn't anticipate this mess and ruin your wedding."

"You didn't ruin anything. What happened wasn't your fault," she told him firmly.

He shrugged and winced. "Maybe not, but having someone try to kill me can't have been on your wish list for the day."

She managed a half-smile. "No, it wasn't, but you mean a great deal to me and so many other people. Seeing you hurt that way was awful, but as Camille said, 'we'd had the best parts by then.'"

He let out a shuddering breath. "I'm so glad you feel that way." Luke was clearly suffering, and it wasn't just from the knife wound.

"Did the detective give you a hard time?"

"I tried to be reasonable."

The voice behind her made Maddie turn her head so

fast, she was in danger of whiplash. "I thought you'd gone, Detective Jones."

"You hoped I'd gone," he corrected and leaned against the door frame. "I'm sure you've got plenty of questions for Luke, but he is the major witness in an ongoing investigation, so I'll thank you to keep them to yourself."

Maddie pouted. "You can't mean that."

His eyebrow smashed into his hairline. "I would think you know by now I don't say anything I don't mean."

This was true, if darn annoying, and she tapped her thigh. "Fine. If you don't want my help, I won't discuss the attempted murder at my wedding."

Jones's mouth twitched. "Much appreciated."

"How's Beth?" Luke might have lost a good deal of blood, but his cheeks suddenly found some of what he did have left.

Maddie watched the heart monitor rise. "She was naturally upset, but I haven't heard from her since I left."

"She's at the station in Maple Falls," Jones informed them.

Maddie gasped. "What for?"

Luke lifted his head. "I tried to tell him that she had nothing to do with the stabbing, but he said it was standard since she was the only witness."

Maddie gently pushed him back to the pillow. "It's okay. They won't keep her long when they realize she didn't see anything."

"Ms. Flynn...," Jones warned.

"It's Mrs. Tanner," she corrected. "I only meant that it wasn't possible for her to stab Luke if he didn't see her as he was stabbed in the front. Plus, she was seen coming from the bathroom at the time Luke was stabbed."

"So I heard." Steve's voice was chilly. "That doesn't make it a fact."

Maddie blinked. "You're calling Gran a liar?"

His mouth gaped for a moment before it snapped shut. "Not at all. However, the timing could be out a couple of minutes, which would make all the difference to what happened. Besides, Beth may have seen someone at the scene and not clicked about the relevance when she gave her statement."

"Beth isn't stupid," Luke growled.

The detective's nostrils flared. "That remains to be seen, since we know that she has been involved in crimes before."

"Hah," Maddie scoffed. "If being blamed with a crime was all a person needed to do to be found guilty, then I'd be serving quite a few sentences myself."

Jones snorted, then looked annoyed. "That's true. However, I didn't say she's been blamed for anything. I'm merely stating that due to her past and that she was at the scene of the crime, she is a person of interest."

"I guess that means you didn't find the weapon yet?"

He pushed off the wall and took a menacing step forward. "I thought you came to see how your friend was?"

Maddie blinked. "I did."

"Then how about you use whatever time you have here asking him about that?"

Her head hung. She was doing it again—putting the crime first.

Luke put his free hand out to her. "I know you're here because you care. Solving the crimes is all part of that and I have faith in your ability to make this right."

The detective didn't say a thing and Maddie didn't look at him.

"Thank you. I do care, Luke, and so do plenty of other

people. I don't know if they told you—there's a full waiting room out there hanging out to hear you're going to be okay. Beth was desperate to come too."

Luke's cheeks pinked again. "I asked her to meet me on the patio because I listened to what you said in your vows about not wasting time. I thought I'd ask Beth if we should make our relationship official. She's shy about all that sort of stuff because of dating my brother." He shot a look at the detective. "People have long memories around here."

"Good for you. We all like Beth, and I saw her face as she tried to stop the bleeding. In fact, the doctor said she saved your life. She was terrified you were going to die. We all were. But we also know you're a fighter."

"Wow! I didn't know that." His grin turned earnest as he put a hand on her arm. "Will you make sure she's okay? Like you wanted to do for Laura when she was falsely accused?"

Jones coughed in the corner.

Maddie kept her gaze on Luke. "Of course I will, but I want you to do something for me. If you do get released later tonight, I think you should go home with Gran."

Eyes turning panicked, he dropped his hand to the bed. "I can't do that."

"You can't go home by yourself, and we both know your parents are away. It's just one night—to make sure you don't have any complications arising from the shock of it all. Please."

"I'll be fine. In case you haven't noticed, I'm all grown up."

Maddie laughed. "I've noticed, but Gran's determined, and you know she always gets her way."

He managed a wry laugh. "She certainly does. I guess one night would be okay, if she doesn't mind."

"Don't be silly. She thinks of you as the grandson she never had."

The blush of surprise was sweet, and Luke was dumbfounded.

Detective Jones coughed again. "I'm not sure the sheriff would approve."

Maddie blinked in confusion and faced him. "Why would Ethan have a problem with Luke staying a night at Gran's?"

"I imagine, he'd think it's a risk when the person responsible for Luke being here could still be hanging around Maple Falls."

He didn't add "to finish the job," but it was certainly implied by his tone. Maddie's fingers drummed on her thighs. "I guess it is a risk, but surely wherever Luke goes, you'll be offering some protection?"

He raised an eyebrow. "If I didn't know better, and that it was impossible for you to see this outcome, I'd think this little scenario was all part of your plan."

She blinked again. "What plan?"

"To put yourself smack in the middle of our investigation."

"Have you forgotten this is my wedding night?"

He rolled his eyes at her indignation. "Not much has stopped you from interfering in a case before today, so I can't see how that would. Besides, the sheriff will be busy for a while yet, so you can't be in a hurry to...." He blushed.

"Begin our honeymoon?" she offered, straight-faced.

Jones's cheeks grew redder than she'd ever seen them, and by the way he huffed and avoided her gaze, Maddie suspected blushing was something he was not used to. His relief was palpable when the nurse came in a moment later and asked Maddie to leave.

It was an issue not being family and she didn't feel the urge to press things while Steve watched over Luke. What she did need was her new husband to spare a minute to check in with her.

While she wanted to help solve the case, she was beginning to worry about Ethan. Yes, he was busy, but he was working on an attempted murder case, which meant he might be the one in danger.

And, perhaps a little selfishly, she was beginning to wonder if a honeymoon was likely anytime soon.

Chapter Thirty-Four

Back in the waiting room, Maddie updated the group on Luke's progress. "I told him about your offer, and he's agreed to come stay for one night."

Gran smiled. "Good work. I was worried with him being so independent, that he'd say no."

"He did at first and it didn't help that Steve Jones didn't want him to. He's worried, and thinks Ethan would be, too, about the attacker coming back to finish the job."

"He can try," Gran huffed.

"Don't you start getting feisty," Maddie warned.

"I don't intend to, but I will protect my own."

Maddie gave her a hug. "Can I suggest that you all go home, and I'll wait for Luke to be discharged?"

"But it's your honeymoon," Laura protested.

"Yeah, I think we can safely say that it's been postponed until Ethan and his deputies find the killer." It was simply the truth, and though the others accepted this, the look of pity in their eyes was almost too much for Maddie. It was the reality of living in a small town where it was all-hands-on-deck when something big occurred. You couldn't get much bigger than murder and it would feel just as personal to other people in Maple Falls as it did to her.

"What a shame." Angel gave her a quick hug. "I guess this is how it will always be for you two, so it isn't a surprise. You really think it's the same person, sugar?"

"I'm pretty sure it is."

Suzy yawned. "Come on, you lot. We won't get to see Luke, so we may as well do as Maddie says. Let's go home."

"Y'all go on ahead and make sure Gran and Laura are locked up safe and sound." Angel waved at the door. "I'll stay with Maddie."

"You don't have to do that," she protested.

Angel winked. "The chief bridesmaid always stays until the end."

"I didn't know that."

"That's because you've never been married before and I eloped, so you couldn't do it for me."

"Next time, then." Maddie nudged her.

Angel clasped a hand to her chest in horror. "Don't hold your breath."

They walked the others to the door and hugged it out.

Camille hung back. "Could I have a word, Maddie?"

"Sure, what's up?"

"Want me to give you two some privacy?" Angel asked. "I can step outside."

"No, it's okay. I've been sitting here thinking about the wedding and how it was so wonderful that you invited so many people from the town. People you've talked about for years."

Maddie nodded, not sure where this was going.

"Watching people coming and going in this waiting room made me think about the man I saw outside the church who wasn't exactly dressed up. In fact, he wore a black outfit and seemed to be trying to stay out of sight."

This was news to Maddie. They were in the middle of a wedding at the time and Camille didn't know everyone who might be attending. However, for Camille to even imagine something wasn't right made Maddie's skin prickle. "Did you mention this to Ethan?"

Her friend nodded. "He thanked me, but since I never saw his face, I knew what I had to say was nothing much to go on. Only, I was listening to you all talk about that singer's death and how the murder still wasn't solved and I got to thinking how odd it was that the man I saw today was wearing cowboy boots."

Angel shrugged. "That's nothing strange around here, sugar."

"Maybe, but would you wear them if you wanted to blend in at a wedding?"

"Perhaps he was nearby, and hearing the bells, decided to be nosey," Maddie suggested without conviction.

Camille tilted her head. "You're probably right. Anyway, I better get out to the car before I miss my ride."

Maddie paced around one half of the room, avoiding the other people who, like them, were waiting on news of a loved one. The place was considerably quieter without the rest of their group, and Angel had gone back to the magazines.

What if Camille was right? Buddy wore a Stetson and cowboy boots. Barney's Bar had been filled with men wearing similar attire and most wore cowboy boots. She'd had the nagging feeling that the answer lay at the bar, but where exactly?

If only Hugo hadn't disappeared.

She stopped in the middle of the room. Disappeared?

Was that Hugo's choice? What if someone had seen him speak to Maddie and they'd considered he'd said too much? It was a coincidence that rang the alarm bells that she knew meant something. But Ethan wasn't answering her calls and Detective Jones wasn't willing to engage with her. Who could she tell?

Sparkling blue eyes edged with weariness watched her from across the room and a delicate eyebrow arched in question.

Maddie sat beside her friend. The one who always listened to her, even when she didn't approve of her penchant for digging into crimes. "We need to find out what happened to Hugo. I think his sudden disappearance could be crucial to finding the killer."

Angel rolled her eyes. "One look at your face told me this night wasn't over by a long shot. What's the plan? We get Luke settled at Gran's and then we head back to Barney's?"

"No way can we go there tonight." Maddie sighed. "Besides the bar being closed by the time we get Luke home, Ethan would have a king-sized fit, not to mention Steve."

Angel nodded. "That's true. So how are we going to get the information we need?"

Maddie slumped back in the chair and closed her eyes. "Right now, I have no idea." A hand covered hers and she grasped it.

"Look, I know you want to make this right," Angel said gently, "but whatever you decide, you are not to go off on your own. Okay."

"Okay." Maddie leaned her head on Angel's shoulder. "I get that I sound desperate, and it's selfish to involve you. I don't want any more of my friends hurt because of this business."

"You could never be selfish." Angel nudged her. "A little hyper-focused maybe."

Maddie managed a small chuckle. "You have a way of grounding me."

"That's my job," Angel asserted.

"Well, thank you anyway. It was good of you to stay with me tonight."

"Like I say—just part of my job. One I would take any day and not just as your bridesmaid." Angel suddenly frowned. "Plus, there is Beth to consider. If they charge her, I'll pay for a lawyer."

Maddie shook her head. "I can't see how they can charge her for anything. I saw what she did to save Luke and no one could fake that level of fear and worry."

"I know how it was, and how it looked, but the law can be funny when you have history."

There was a terseness to Angel's comment that Maddie understood. Beth had been involved in a crime against her will and she'd paid her dues. "Thanks to you giving her a chance, Beth's shaping up to be a good hairdresser and has turned her life around. She's a good friend to Luke. And I can't imagine her hurting him."

"I agree, but I saw Steve's face when he saw her leaning over Luke, and I don't think he'd agree with us. Mind you, he was grumpy all day, and really annoyed me, so maybe I'm reading more into it."

Maddie couldn't agree more with this take on the detective, but sensed her friend had something to say. "What did he do to annoy you?"

"I could write a list, but it was when I had to drag him onto the dance floor and then he wouldn't say a word unless it was to answer my questions. Words like, *fine, yes,* and *no*. I mean, what got stuck up his butt to be like that with me?"

"Did you expect more?"

Angel pursed her lips. "More than civility, for sure. The last few times we saw each other I thought we had a connection and even an understanding that we might try to get to know each other better."

Though they hadn't seen each other in a while, it had been obvious whenever the two of them were together that there was something between the detective and Angel and Maddie felt the need to tread carefully. "That was months ago when we had all the drama with Camille's fiancé getting killed and you haven't spoken about Steve since then. I assumed you'd changed your mind. Have you tried to contact him at all?"

"Of course I did," Angel scoffed. "I'm not exactly shy. He's been ghosting me."

Maddie gasped, unable to believe she hadn't known this was going on with her best friend. "Really? Why didn't you tell me?"

Angel shrugged. "I was angry and frankly, embarrassed."

"Why were you embarrassed? Did you say something weird?"

"Sugar, that's almost a given."

Maddie snorted. "Like what?"

"Good grief. As if I had a clue. Anyway, the man knows what I'm like and he was keen before, so something's turned him off the idea of us being friends in any way. Again, I have no idea what that could be, but that's just how it is."

Angel may come across as not interested in having a boyfriend, but Maddie should have noticed earlier that her friend was hurt by Steve's attitude and that there was still something there. Otherwise, Angel wouldn't be talking about it. "I really think there's more to this than meets the eye and a conversation needs to be had."

"He had his chance and let's just say that conversation is not his strong point," Angel huffed.

As if she'd summoned him, the hulking detective strode into the waiting room with Luke, who still looked far too pale.

"I'm escorting Luke to Gran's, so you may as well come with me," he told them gruffly.

The women stood.

"Thank you," Maddie said without conferring with her friend.

Angel sniffed and without a word, walked stiffly out the door.

Chapter Thirty-Five

The drive back to Maple Falls was very quiet. Luke leaned against the passenger door of the dark sedan and Angel stared out the side window behind him. Maddie noted that the detective kept glancing in the rearview mirror at Angel. His eyes met Maddie's a couple of times, and he immediately looked ahead.

She sighed as she sent a message to Gran. It seemed that the path of love in Maple Falls was convoluted for all its inhabitants and stretched further afield.

With the tense atmosphere and worry over Luke, the light over Gran's porch was a welcome sight.

Steve helped Luke from the car and up the path to where the others waited. Gran took charge by ushering them all into the sitting room. "You should go straight to bed, young man."

Luke nodded. "I will, if you don't mind."

"Mind. I mind everything that's happened, son, but having you here is not an issue, and just you remember that."

He smiled weakly and Gran issued more orders,

"Detective, you get him into bed. Up the stairs and the last room on your right. It was Maddie's room, so don't mind all the pink. I found a pair of pajamas that should do for one night. There's water beside the bed, and I've left you a sandwich, Luke. I made it fresh when Maddie messaged you were on your way. Please say if you want something else to eat. Maddie and Angel, sit down before you fall. Laura, make some tea, please."

Everyone obeyed without question, and a few minutes later, Steve came downstairs, having to duck a little on the lower part of the ceiling. "I persuaded Luke to put the pajamas on and he's settled."

"Hopefully the pajamas don't smell of mothballs. They were my husband's, and I forgot they were there until I went hunting for something suitable."

"He didn't complain, but he wasn't hungry."

"That's fine. We'll make sure he eats something when he wakes up. Take a seat, Steve."

Almost down the hall, he turned. "I should wait outside."

"Wait for what? The killer?" Maddie asked, then, when she saw the shadow cross his features, wished she hadn't.

"I think after the day's events, it's not worth leaving anything to chance," he said soberly.

Gran sighed. "It sounds like you're planning on a long night. Laura will get you some coffee."

"Hopefully the sheriff will send someone to relieve me soon." Steve took a seat but hesitated before accepting the coffee from Laura.

"She's hardly going to poison you in front of us," Angel growled.

He blinked at her. "I didn't think she would."

"Sure you didn't. It's obvious you think we're all in

cahoots in this murder and doing what we can to mess things up instead of being the meek little doormats you'd prefer."

Steve frowned as if he didn't understand, and Maddie, thinking it best to let the two of them sort their issues out privately, got up and headed to the kitchen. "I might make some sandwiches."

Laura had already slunk out of the room and all except Angel followed them.

"Goodness, you can cut the tension with a knife." Camille peered round the door at the two remaining. "Surely that can't have anything to do with Luke?"

"No. This is something those two need to work through and it's incredibly bad timing," Maddie explained. "I had an idea that I wanted to discuss with the detective, but I don't think it's worth bringing up now that Angel has him in her sights."

"If it can help the case, maybe you need to, regardless of what it's about," Laura whispered over Gran's shoulder. "This could get ugly."

"What's your problem?" Steve's growl came through clearly from the other room.

"Excuse me?" Angel's angry voice was even louder. "You're the one who treats me and my family with disdain."

"I don't know what you're talking about. I think I'm polite enough," Steve protested.

"Really?" Angel scoffed. "At the wedding, you didn't want to touch me, let alone dance with me."

Steve groaned. "That's what this is about? I don't like dancing, and you know I don't like public displays of affection."

"Said almost every man ever!" Angel retorted. "I hoped you were different and didn't conform to a stereotype because you're smarter than that. Clearly, I was wrong."

"Do something," Laura begged. When Gran nodded, Maddie, exhausted and wanting desperately for this day to be over, and having already decided things had gone far enough, edged into the sitting room.

Steve scratched his head. "I am so lost right now; I can't even think how to respond."

Maddie coughed to get their attention. "Steve, Angel likes you and she thought you liked her."

He faced Maddie with a frown. "Of course I like her."

"Not *like* like," Angel retorted, then waved a hand. "Never mind. Just forget it."

Steve leaned toward Angel; his gaze glued to her face. "I thought you understood that when I'm working, I have to act a certain way."

That eyebrow Angel used to great effect hit her hairline. "Oh, you were working at the wedding?"

His frown deepened. "Well, yes. Someone had to look out for Ethan and Maddie in case the crime was connected to them. It made sense for that someone to be me. Why did you think I was in the wedding party?"

At this stage, Maddie was pretty sure everyone's mouth was gaping like hers. "I thought it was because the two of you were friends."

Angel nodded. "Me too."

"That's how it was supposed to look. I mean, we are friendly. Anyway, I just assumed Ethan would tell you, Maddie."

She blinked several times as she considered this. There had clearly been a lot of assumptions made, including Maddie's acceptance over Ethan's choice of groomsmen. With his childhood friends having moved away, he'd been short of choice and picking Steve had seemed logical. Just not in the way she'd thought.

"I still think you could have looked happy about dancing with me," Angel muttered.

The tips of his ears reddened. "It took a lot not to enjoy holding you," he muttered right back.

It took barely a second before Angel suddenly grinned as if the whole angry drama was an act. "Aha! I knew it."

Relief slipped over his features, and he chuckled. "No, you didn't," he teased. "I'm a great detective."

Maddie groaned and shook her head at her friend. "Seriously? You were baiting him just now?"

Angel shrugged, but her eyes twinkled. "I can't abide mixed messages, and I had no idea he was in detective mode, but I just had a feeling there was more to it than him having a change of heart." She turned to Steve. "I wracked my brain thinking of what I could have done wrong and why you were suddenly treating me the way Rob was treating Laura."

His smile was earnest. "You didn't do anything, and I honestly think Rob is mad at himself for not stepping in when he saw Laura with Buddy. I guess he's taking some blame for the death by punishing himself."

Laura edged into the room her eyes wide. "Really?"

He coughed, perhaps just realizing how open he was being. "Obviously, I don't know that for sure."

Suzy snapped her fingers "That makes so much sense. I heard him talking to his dogs about how stupid he was. When he saw me behind him, he was pretty embarrassed."

"But he was so awful to Laura," Angel reminded her. "What excuses that?"

"Rob was told what to do, and he was trying to do a professional job despite his feelings. I guess he took it too far, but it's not easy to keep the lines from blurring when you get involved with civilians." Steve looked pointedly at Angel.

"Ethan's always reminding me of that." Maddie took a risk and took a step closer to Steve. "You're going to get angry, but please hear me out. I have a theory."

He glanced around the room with something like resignation at being outnumbered, which he totally was.

Chapter Thirty-Six

The detective sighed and leaned back. "I'm listening."

Maddie licked her lips and told him what she thought. "Hugo loved his job, and he wouldn't disappear without good reason."

"We've looked into it, but there were no records of him taking a cab, train, or plane. We have no credit cards in his name being used at those places or at gas stations either."

"There you go," Maddie said excitedly. "Unless he had unlimited cash, and who does these days, if he left of his own accord, there would have to be some trail to indicate the mode of transportation. What I don't think you've considered was how open Hugo was when discussing Buddy's issues with substance abuse. Maybe he discussed it with others, but his disappearance happened so soon after our visit. If the wrong person heard him talking to us, he could have been in danger from that moment. It could also explain how we were suddenly involved—aside from Laura having one date with him."

"All right, I'll bite." Steve shrugged. "Where do you think Hugo is?"

Though it was obvious to her, Maddie grimaced at saying so. "He's dead."

The other women gasped.

"He has to be if drug dealers wanted him silenced permanently," Maddie told them reasonably. "Since Hugo is nowhere to be found and you have no credit card trail of him showing up anywhere else, I believe his body must still be in Destiny and, because he wasn't a small man, I think two people are involved. Just like they were in Buddy's case."

Steve pursed his lips. "I can see how you'd come to your conclusion, but these are still guesses."

"She's usually right, though, isn't she?" Gran asked.

"You can say what you like about being a guess, but my daughter has scarily accurate instincts and she thinks things through in a very in-depth way," her mom interjected. "Just like my father. If Maddie says that's a likely scenario, then it has to be worth looking into. Don't you think?"

Steve stood. "Let me make a call. For the record, I'm not promising anything."

"Good man. Now, we need to get you girls to bed. Ava, you'd better share with me. Suzy and Camille can share with Laura as that room is a decent size, which leaves Maddie and Angel in the small room at the front of the house."

"I should get home, Gran," Suzy protested.

"No one is leaving here tonight. I want to know you're all safe, and since we have our own guard on duty, this is the best place."

Angel shrugged. "Since I'm sure the offer comes with breakfast, I'm okay with it."

One by one, they washed up and got into the night-gowns Gran and Laura provided. It made Maddie smile to think of Gran and Ava sharing a bed after spending so much time apart.

Steve came back in briefly to tell them he had someone checking places of interest for Hugo and that he would be patrolling the cottage. Gran made him a flask of coffee and after much yawning from everyone, they locked the doors and headed up to bed.

Angel lay facing Maddie in the pullout sofa bed in what was supposed to be the formal sitting room, which no one used as they all preferred the coziness of the open plan rooms by the kitchen.

"Sharing a bed with you brings back good memories. You doing okay, sugar?"

"Yeah." Maddie sighed. "It's been a very long day, though, and hasn't quite ended the way I'd hoped."

Angel squeezed her hand. "I'm so sorry about the wedding night. And everything else."

A lump formed in Maddie's throat. "Me too. Let's just try to sleep."

Angel nodded and yawned. "Things will be better in the morning. Night, night."

Maddie lay in the dark, watching the shadows on the wall. The clock by the bed clicked over to midnight and though she was exhausted, sleep wasn't even close. Something dark loomed over her and she couldn't shake the feeling of dread. Even the knowledge that Steve was on patrol didn't help. When Angel began to breathe deeply, she got up and pulled on a sweatshirt over the nightie. Perhaps some hot chocolate would help.

Slipping out into the hall, she checked her phone to find a message.

"I'm fine and so relieved you're at Gran's with Steve. Stay safe and I'll see you in the morning. Love you."

Maddie's heart warmed a little. Despite everything, the message was a good start to their marriage. He'd kept his promise to let her know he was okay.

A shadow drifted across the window in the kitchen and a face peered in at her. She smiled and pointed to the range where she'd put the pot of milk to boil. Steve smiled back and shook his head.

Things had a funny way of working out. As long as her friends and family were safe, she was happy. A thump behind her heralded Big Red, who sashayed into the kitchen and yawned.

"Sorry to wake you, buddy."

He tilted his head before looking at his bowl.

"It's nowhere near breakfast time and I'm sure Gran fed you plenty last night."

He gave her a filthy look and was turning away when he stopped, one paw comically in midair. Then Maddie heard it too. A muffled cry. Outside.

She waited for several heartbeats. Surely if Steve had found someone bent on trouble, he would bring them to the house. Or would he simply march them to the police station?

Unless he was the one surprised....

Unable to bear not knowing, Maddie took a poker from the fireplace and gingerly unlocked the back door. Opening it as quietly as possible, she slipped outside. Big Red immediately darted toward the small shed near the hen house. With no footwear, Maddie moved silently, one slow step at a time.

A grunt came from around the other side of the building

and a few of the chickens nearby began to cluck. Hugging the wood on the back wall, she peered around the right-hand side. There was no one visible, yet the grunting grew louder. At the next corner, she paused before darting a glance around it.

A man dragged a body inside the shed. While she wasn't a hundred percent certain the figure on the ground was Steve, Maddie couldn't think of another scenario where it wouldn't be. Not when the man doing the hauling had a cover over his face. When the man was about to close the door, Maddie took her opportunity.

Racing toward him, she raised the poker. He must have seen her shadow move as he lifted his head just in time. She recognized Eric's cold eyes before his arm reached toward her, taking the brunt of the impact. He yelped but barely hesitated as he rushed toward her.

Maddie crouched low, which helped when he threw her to the ground. The natural reflex to knee his groin had him crumple on top of her, which wasn't so good. He was a big man. And he wasn't alone.

"What the heck is going on?"

The stage whisper sounded familiar, but she was wheezing herself and couldn't be sure of much as the man standing dragged the other one off her. Their eyes met and he glared down at her.

"I should have known. You've been trouble since day one," he growled.

"Really? I'm terribly sorry to interfere with your murder and attempted murder."

"You should be," he snarled at her sarcasm. "You've cost me a lot of money."

"Me?" she asked innocently.

Ignoring her now that the other man was upright, he

checked that Steve was shut in the shed. "Did he see your face?"

"I don't think so," Eric replied nervously. "I hit him from behind."

The second man turned back to Maddie. "Then I guess that just leaves you."

"I can't see your face in this light," she protested as her stomach churned.

"Maybe not, but you know who I am, right?"

Of all the times to not be able to lie, this had to be the worst. "I can't say I'm certain."

He actually laughed. "Yeah, that's not quite enough for me to let you go and you're not a good liar."

Her voice squeaked annoyingly. "So you're going to murder me too, Barney?"

He glanced up at the house. "I honestly wish I didn't have to, but you have no idea what you've got involved in."

"You must mean the drugs?" she blurted. Which was not the smartest thing she'd ever done, but she didn't like to think what he was going to do after he'd dealt with her.

His eyes drilled into hers. "What do you know about that?"

He was intimidating, but now it didn't feel like there was anything to lose by pushing for more information. "Admittedly not much, but enough to say that Buddy must have upset all your plans when he decided to go straight."

"That's putting it mildly. However, we reached a deal that he would keep quiet about everything, and I trusted him. Right up until his impromptu date. The redhead has something I need."

Maddie couldn't help the gasp of horror escaping. "Whatever it is, she has no idea about any of this."

"While I'd like to believe you, that doesn't seem likely."

He eyed her curiously. "Do you know what I'm looking for?"

Maddie was no stranger to stalling for time and it had just occurred to her that if Steve was supposed to have someone come relieve him soon, that was her best hope for getting out of this alive. And not just her. There was a house full of people she loved behind her, and she would do anything to protect them. "I wish I did. Can I ask you a question?"

"I bet you say that a lot to that new husband of yours." He smirked. "Shame you won't get to enjoy a honeymoon. Ever."

Anger rose red and orange. If he touched a hair on Ethan's head, she didn't know what she would do, but she would hurt him bad. Although, that could be a moot point, she realized, and took a deep breath to calm herself. Grandad always said, anger and panic were what got you into trouble fastest. "Was putting Buddy in the chiller just a way to get more time?"

"You are smart. I'll give you that. I needed an alibi. Therefore, Buddy had to disappear for several hours."

"Boss, we should get out of here," Eric interjected.

"Not until I have what I came for." He looked down at Maddie. "Time is running out for all of us, but I aim to deliver."

Deliver? Maddie searched her mind for something that Laura could have gotten from Buddy in the short time they were together. As far as she knew, it could only be one thing. "The Stetson."

"Give the little lady a prize," the big man said dryly. "Now get up and come over here so you can keep the detective company."

She knew there wasn't much time before he killed her,

and the odds of another deputy coming soon were slim. How would he do it? A gunshot would be too noisy at this time of night when the town was quiet, and the police station wasn't that far away. A knife in the ribs, like Buddy? Or would he break her neck? Barney and his accomplice looked capable of either.

Scrambling inelegantly to her feet, Maddie felt the edge of a broken brick under her palm and, using the side of the building for leverage, threw it at his face with everything she had.

He ducked but the side of it scraped his cheek. She backed away as fast as she could.

"You'll pay for that," he growled, striding toward her.

Chapter Thirty-Seven

Maddie bent into a fighting stance. She was all that was standing in the way of this monster getting to her family, and fear didn't have a place right now. Eyes narrowed, she waited for him to initiate the fight.

He reached out to grab her and she brought the side of her hand down on his wrist. When he took a second to shake it off, she swept her leg under his and he toppled back. Ready to attack, she was hauled into the air.

Darn, she'd forgotten about Eric who must have gone around the other side of the shed. She kicked out and a curse rang out. Ethan?

"Get back!" he ordered.

She stumbled as he pushed her behind him, never happier to see anyone than in that moment.

"Stay down and spread your arms out!"

The man hesitated, anger warring with defeat before he complied, and Ethan knelt on his back while he cuffed him.

"There's another man around somewhere," Maddie called from the back door, which she was determined to guard. Big Red sat beside her as they scanned the yard. "I'm pretty sure there are only two of them."

"Don't worry about him. Rob already dealt with the other guy."

Relief washed over her as Ethan hauled the man to his feet, though her skin prickled once more when Big Red ran down the steps toward the shed.

"Look who I found." Rob came around the corner, pushing the other cuffed offender in front of him while the groggy detective leaned on Rob's shoulder.

"Good work." Ethan turned to Maddie. "Can you take care of Steve while Rob and I get these two around to the station?"

"Of course. I'll call the paramedics, just to be sure he's okay." Maddie took over from Rob and helped Steve into the cottage. The detective clung to her, which showed how badly the knock had affected him.

Lights glared when Gran came into the kitchen and flicked the switch. "Goodness, Steve looks terrible. What's going on?"

"I think he'll be fine. Could you get an icepack for his head?" Maddie sat the detective in Gran's comfy chair, and he leaned back with a sigh.

Gran quickly did as she was asked and came back with the icepack just as Angel made an entrance. How she managed to look like she'd been up for hours instead of a mess like Maddie was a mystery.

Angel's eyes widened at the pale detective and dropping to her knees beside him, she grabbed his hand. "Sugar, what on earth has happened?"

"Put this on his head. He's taken a blow there." Gran handed her the icepack and backed away with a look of satisfaction.

Angel took the pack and pulling his head toward her, gently put the pack in place and pushed him back but kept her hand there.

Steve wasn't his usual dismissive self, so he clearly wasn't right. Leaving him in capable hands, Maddie phoned the paramedics from the kitchen.

Gran was already making tea when the rest of the cottage's inhabitants descended.

Her mom, arrived first, ushering the other women into the room. "Poor Steve. It looks like he has a terrible headache and the last thing he needs is all of us fussing around him." Her gaze swept over Maddie. "I don't know how we slept through whatever's been going on here, but I'd hazard a guess that you've been outside fighting, haven't you?"

Suzy looked her over. "Is that mud on your nightie and sweatshirt."

Maddie glanced down at her clothes. "Probably. We had two intruders, and one attacked the detective. Big Red alerted me to the danger."

"So you went outside to fight them?" Laura almost hyperventilated.

"Not exactly," Maddie explained. "I was worried about Steve being out there on his own. One minute I could see him and the next minute he was gone and then I heard a noise."

Camille tutted. "You could have been killed."

"We all could have," Maddie pointed out. "They were determined to get to Laura, and I couldn't let them get inside. Not with Luke being injured and the rest of you asleep. I hate to think what they might have done if one of you had woken up and confronted them."

Gran shook her head. "That's very noble of you, dear,

and I know I shouldn't be so shocked, what with your grand-dad's shenanigans, but I'll never get used to you getting involved in these cases so physically."

"That's exactly how I feel about this." Her mom sighed. "I don't know whether to slap my daughter for being reckless or hug her for saving the day—yet again."

"I get it, and I promise that I don't particularly relish getting into a fight." Maddie flushed a little as she recalled the man dropping to his knees in front of her. "But to be honest, I did derive some satisfaction after they disrupted my wedding day and hurt Luke."

"And killed Buddy," Laura added, then frowned. "You said they wanted to get to me. What did I do to make them so intent on that?"

"You have something that they desperately want. Something Buddy intended to keep out of their hands. No matter what."

"What could I possibly have of Buddy's?"

Maddie tilted her head and watched the realization dawn in her friend's eyes.

Laura gasped. "You can't mean the Stetson?"

Maddie nodded.

"But if it was so important, they only had to ask, and I would have gladly given it to them." Laura clasped her hands together. "Why would they kill for a hat?"

Gran put her arm around Laura's shoulders. "Think about it, dear. He gave it to you for safe keeping. I don't think he imagined that what happened next would come about so soon."

"That's right," Maddie agreed. "Buddy likely thought he would see you again soon. Why don't you go get the Stetson?"

"Shouldn't we wait for Steve to feel a little better?"

Laura asked. "I mean, should we even be touching it if it holds clues?"

A siren wailed nearby, and car lights shone done the hallway.

"You could wait, but then it's unlikely we'll find out everything once you hand it over," Suzy declared. "Once you do, we'll be waiting a long time for the truth to come out."

While Laura dithered, Gran pulled open a drawer and plucked a pair of plastic gloves from inside. She handed them to Maddie. "You all go upstairs and wait for me while I let the paramedics in."

It wasn't by the book, yet Maddie wasn't an officer of the law, and she could no more ignore her curiosity than Suzy and Gran. Taking the gloves, she stuffed them in her pocket and along with the others, sidled through the sitting room and up the stairs.

They entered Laura's room where Suzy and her mom perched on the bed.

Laura opened her wardrobe and pointed at the Stetson. "It was already dusted for fingerprints and it only had mine and Buddy's, so they gave it back to me when they let me go. Surely if there was anything concealed in it, the police would have found it."

"Well, you best get it down and put it on the bed so we can all see," Gran said as she came through the doorway.

Maddie handed Laura the gloves, but she backed away. "You do it."

Naturally, her fingers were itching to do exactly that, so Maddie pulled on the gloves and retrieved the hat. Sitting beside her mom, she ran her fingers around the brim. It was smooth all the way with no bumps. Next, she put her fingers into the top, stroking each indentation.

"There really is no room to conceal anything," she muttered and turned her attention to the band inside. Split into five pieces, with one sporting a small ribbon, which denoted the back, she gently prized each piece up. One immediately flopped back down, and her breath caught in her throat.

Suzy peered over her shoulder. "What did you find?"

Tugging something loose from the fabric, she held up her hand. "A key. A very small key."

"Madeline Tanner! Get your butt down here, right now!" Her husband's voice boomed from downstairs, making everyone in the room stiffen.

"It's Ethan, and he doesn't sound happy," Laura commented unnecessarily.

Wincing, and with all eyes on her, Maddie carried the Stetson downstairs. Obviously, the two killers had confessed a little earlier than she'd anticipated. On one hand, Ethan's tone was worrying, while on the other, hearing her married name did give her a little thrill.

Chapter Thirty-Eight

Twenty-four hours later, the group reconvened at the cottage. Tired and relieved that the criminals had been caught, there was still some confusion over several clues that hadn't tied in with the murder.

After Gran and Laura poured coffee and tea for their guests, and Maddie set out plates of food, Angel kicked off the discussion.

"I still find it hard to understand. If they were such good friends, why did Eric kill Buddy?"

Steve sighed, and he took the cup of coffee she handed to him. "Jealousy and drugs. Those two things alone ruin so many lives."

"There must be more to it," Suzy asserted.

Maddie looked to Ethan, who nodded. "The truth was, Buddy upset several people. When his relationship with his wife broke, he blamed himself for putting his career first. It was only after she left him that he realized what was the most important thing in his life. Broken and hurting, the drugs helped—or so he thought. Then he met Luke."

Everyone turned to face the young man who blushed.

"He told me about the pitfalls of his career but didn't speak about his wife."

"But it sounds like whatever you did say affected him positively," Gran told him.

Luke shrugged, wincing as his hand held his side. "I only spoke of my passion for baking and how my father had ridiculed me. Having the same experience, plus his drive to be successful, came at a huge cost, because he could never get enough."

"Enough of what, dear?"

"Fame and money." Luke sighed. "He thought if he had those things, his father would accept that he was successful. It didn't work, but Buddy couldn't accept that. Not back then."

Laura sniffed. "How sad."

"It's all terribly tragic, but I'd like to hear about the key." Maddie faced Ethan. "It's where it all began if I'm not mistaken."

Ethan smiled. "Are you ever? The key was to a safety deposit box in Destiny. Buddy had a little black book. Literally. Names, dates, times of drug deals that Barney was involved in. It was all there."

"But how did you know who the culprits were?" Angel asked.

"We didn't for sure. We did get another fingerprint off the cap, but it didn't come up with a match until we caught Eric."

"There was another clue we missed," Maddie noted. "The night of the murder we bumped into a guy at the mouth of the alley. Do you recall?"

Those that had nodded.

"Well that man wore a Stetson very like Buddy's," she continued. "It had a feather attached."

Suzy frowned. "Most do."

"True," Ethan nodded, "but when we searched Eric's place we found his Stetson minus the feather."

"Oh, my goodness!" Angel squealed. "The feather on the floor of the bakery."

"That's right," Steve beamed at her. "DNA proved it."

"The car was another issue, and we located it in a lock-up under Barney's name," Ethan explained. "But it was Maddie who put us on the path when she spoke of Hugo's disappearance. He'd paid rent for another six months, so we knew she was right about him not leaving town. We searched his house and found Hugo's body in the basement."

"Another body?" Laura gasped.

"Here, drink this sweet tea." Gran forced a cup into her hands.

"But how did that lead you to the killers?" Maddie's mom pointed at her watch. "I've got a plane to catch, and Bernie will be here soon."

Gran tutted at her, but Ethan merely smiled.

"Eric had enjoyed a long friendship with Buddy. They'd done drugs together and though Buddy stopped, Eric couldn't hold a job. He began selling drugs for Barney who, thanks to Maddie, won't be doing any more buying or selling for a very long time."

Angel pursed her lips. "You've been holding out on us, Maddie."

"Only their names. Until they were processed, I couldn't share that information." Maddie told them apologetically.

"She's learning," Steve muttered. "Albeit, slowly."

Ethan squeezed her shoulder. "While I hate the fact

that you were in harm's way, I am proud of how you helped the case."

"I won't say I told you so." She smiled, delighted by Ethan's words. "I'm just so glad no one here was hurt. Sorry, except for Luke."

Luke shook his head sadly. "If I hadn't been so caught up, I may have paid more attention to Eric's behavior. He was short with me on more than one occasion, but Buddy said not to mind him—it was just his way."

"And I wish I'd mentioned the man at the wedding earlier," Camille admitted.

"None of this is anyone's fault. Bad people will do bad things no matter what," Gran assured them. "Let's just be grateful that the wedding was amazing and that our family is safe."

"Family?" Steve's eyes twinkled.

"Close friends are as good as family," Gran asserted. "Anyone for tea? I think you'll suit the Moroccan glass set I recently picked up, Steve."

"Sorry, I don't drink tea."

Gran smiled patiently at the detective. "We'll work on that. Meanwhile, you can have coffee in it."

Ethan laughed. "Give in graciously, my friend. It's easier."

"So I've been told." The detective eyed Angel, who winked at him.

Biting back a laugh at the couple, Maddie stood. "Well, as much as this has been 'fun,' and tea is always welcome, I think it's time my husband and I went home."

"I thought you'd postponed the honeymoon indefinitely?" her mom asked.

"We have. That doesn't mean we can't spend an evening together not worrying about anything. Plus, you're leaving and so is Camille. We can see this lot anytime."

Suzy rolled her eyes. "Charming."

Gran laughed. "Why not take the day off tomorrow and leave the baking to Laura and me?"

Laura nodded effusively. "You were going to take a week off for your honeymoon, so you really should take at least a day, if not more."

Maddie shook her head. "Luke will be out for several more days. It's too much for you and Gran."

"Besides, I'm snowed under at work with all the paper-work," Ethan added.

"Just take the day off. Both of you. And stop arguing about it," Steve told them in a no-nonsense way.

Ethan and Maddie shared a look that was more of a question. A day would be nice, wouldn't it?

"Let's do it." Ethan smiled convincingly. "We can go for a drive and spend the night at the house."

Maddie blinked and caught looks from her mom and Gran. He'd said house, not the apartment. Big Red waited at the hall doorway as if it was all decided. And really, what was the issue? She grabbed Ethan's arm, looking meaning-fully at him. "I see I'm outnumbered, so just this once, I'll go with the flow and do what I'm told. Only, it better not be a ruse to get me to change my mind about where our home should be."

Ethan dropped a kiss on the end of her nose. "I would never dare try to trick you, Mrs. Tanner. After all, as an amateur sleuth, you'd see right through me."

"You can bet I will," she teased.

It sounded like her new husband had found a way to accept who she was and just like her honey cake, their union was close to perfection.

If you enjoyed Honey Cake and Homicide I'd love you to leave a review. Plus, by signing up to my newsletter you can get a bonus epilogue! https://dl.bookfunnel.com/3p80253mo7

While you're waiting for the next book in the series, why not check out The Beagle Diner Mysteries. Read on for an excerpt from Book 1 in the series, Beagles Love Cupcake Crimes.

Beagles Love Cupcake Crimes

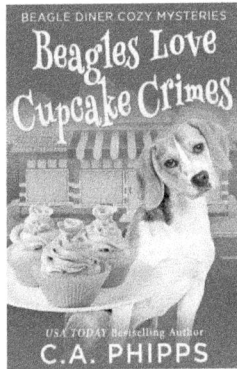

The frosting bag shot from Lyra's hand to land smack on the head of her beagle, where a line of frosting now dripped between caramel-colored eyes. In the blink of those eyes, a long tongue wiped off half the mess.

Lyra St. Claire was in her happy place and unprepared

when her assistant, Maggie Parker, burst into the Portland Hotel suite she often leased.

"Lucky that wasn't chocolate frosting, Mags. Where's the fire?" Lyra stooped to snatch the bag from the furry head. Not that Cinnamon was bothered by that or her sticky fur. The adorable pooch loved cupcakes which was why she sat hopefully at Lyra's feet during the whole process.

The mainly white dog had a brown back, as if a dusting of cinnamon had been poured along her from head to tail. At least the color had been more that shade as a pup. Now her coat was paler—more of a biscuit shade, really—but it was too late to rue that. Besides, Cinnamon sounded far better than Biscuit.

When Lyra looked up again, Maggie was leaning on the kitchen counter. "You're very pale, Mags. Are you ill?"

Maggie shook her head. "I wish there was a right way to tell you this. There's been an accident at the contestants' hotel."

"Did someone get burned?" That would make perfect sense, as it was a cooking contest that Lyra was judging in Boise, and burns were unfortunately frequent in her profession. "Please tell me they're okay."

"If only I could." Maggie grimaced. "Justine Long fell from her balcony. She's dead."

Lyra gasped. "Oh my goodness. Do you know how it happened?"

Maggie shook her head again. "She went back to her room after a practice session. The police are there, but it will take them some time to talk to everybody."

"The rest of the contestants will be in shock. I should get back there and make sure they're okay."

"Your agent was the one who contacted me. Symon also

said to make sure you stayed in Portland. According to him, the police will stop by later. I'm sorry, he didn't give me any more details."

Lyra frowned. "Symon phoned you? Why didn't he contact me?"

Maggie screwed up her nose. "I was surprised too. The contestant's hotel manager called the producer, and he called Symon. Your agent might not have bothered to come on this trip, but you know how tuned in he is to everything that's going on."

Lyra knew exactly what Maggie meant. Symon's finger was firmly on the pulse of every detail of her career—whether she wanted it or not. He should have called her himself, but she couldn't deny it was a relief not to have him around when his presence upset everyone. Including Cinnamon.

Full of reasons for what he expected of her while ignoring her suggestions, she'd bet a strawberry cheesecake he already knew exactly what had happened but was thinking of damage control and not Justine, her family, or the other contestants.

She dialed Symon's number, which clicked to voice mail almost immediately. Clearly she wouldn't get any information from him until he was good and ready, but she desperately needed to know more. She was involved whether he liked it or not, and felt responsible for all the contestants' well-being.

Lyra was well-known as a celebrity chef, and her TV show, *A Lesson with Lyra*, featured guests who were also celebrities. Her platform was the girl-next-door who could teach anyone to cook recipes packed with flavor.

She also hosted regional cooking contests. Boise was the last one and the competition was fierce. After that, the winners of each leg would appear in a grand final held here in Portland. She'd unfortunately had to make the extra trips back and forth to do various pre-show promotions.

Lyra snatched up a cloth and wiped the counter vigorously. "This is tragic. She was so talented, and destined to do well, but I can admit to you that I wasn't particularly fond of Justine. Her abrasive personality made her unpopular with everyone, and sometimes she was downright cruel. I personally witnessed her 'accidentally' knocking other contestants' dishes over on more than one occasion and had to step in." Lyra paused, cloth in hand. "Surely, another contestant didn't have anything to do with her death?"

Maggie frowned. "Do you mean is this a did she fall or was she pushed scenario?"

"Exactly. Because I can't believe Justine would take her own life when she had so much to live for." The words came out a little shaky. "If there was an argument and Justine lost her footing—that's one thing. But what if that wasn't the case?"

"Wow. You think someone wanted retribution? I guess anything's possible." Maggie let that sink in before adding, "We're back there in a few days for the final. I'm sure you'll know more by then either via the papers or if Symon gets in contact."

The counter couldn't be any cleaner, and, needing something to do, Lyra finished frosting the last of the cupcakes. "That's true, although, if it was foul play, they might cancel the rest of the contest."

Leaning over the tray, Maggie followed each swirl with fascination. "They never have after an accident. Then again, no one died before."

"Thank goodness. But however the death happened, it will be hard for the rest of them to continue." Lyra shook her head at her assistant. "I don't know how you can eat, but help yourself. I'll make coffee."

"Food makes me feel better when I'm upset." Maggie grabbed a cupcake and sniffed in appreciation. "Mmmm, chocolate."

Lyra couldn't argue with the reasoning. "Chocolate with a twist. Made especially for you."

Cinnamon, now miraculously clean, padded around the counter to Maggie for a scratch, big eyes glued to the cupcake.

"Poor Cin. I'd give you some if I was allowed."

"She knows she can't have chocolate. Although, it doesn't stop her from wishing I'd drop more than the frosting."

Lyra made coffee, and they sat companionably at the counter.

"These are so good." Maggie nonchalantly reached for a second cupcake.

"I knew you'd love the caramel center, but perhaps you could save one or two for Dan."

Her driver, who did anything else required, would be here soon, and he loved all of Lyra's baking. Between these two, she had discerning taste testers on hand whenever she needed them, and, along with Cinnamon, they took her mind off the troubles which had lately escalated.

Maggie reached for a napkin and dabbed her mouth, the beagle still at her feet in case a few crumbs happened her way. Suddenly, Cinnamon ran to the door, and then a knock sounded. It was Maggie who checked the peephole and admitted the police while Lyra calmed her nerves by wiping the counter some more and making a fresh pot of coffee.

Maggie had done her best to take Lyra's mind off

Justine, but if she were honest, she'd barely been distracted. There were so many unanswered questions, and she hoped the officers had answers.

Want to read more? Pick up your copy of Beagles Love Cupcake Crimes today!

Recipes

These recipes are ones I use all the time and have come down the generations from my mum, grandmother, and some I have adapted from other recipes. Also, I now have my husband's grandmother's recipe book. Exciting! I'll be bringing some of them to life very soon.

Just a wee reminder, that I am a New Zealander. Occasionally I may have missed converting into ounces and pounds for my American readers.

My apologies for that, and please let me know—if you do try them—how they turn out.

Cheryl x

Honey Cake

Honey Cake
Ingredients

1 cup plain flour

1 tsp baking powder

½ tsp salt

¼ tsp ground cinnamon

¼ tsp baking soda

1 cup butter

½ cup brown sugar

4 large eggs

1 tsp vanilla extract

⅓ cup honey plus 3 tablespoons for drizzle when baked

Instructions

1. Preheat oven to 325°F / 160°C. Lightly grease a 9-inch round cake pan with baking spray. Line the bottom with baking paper.

2. In a small bowl, whisk together the flour, baking powder, salt, cinnamon, and baking soda.

3. In a larger bowl beat the butter, sugar, and honey on medium-high until light and fluffy, about 3 minutes. Reduce

speed and add the eggs, one at a time, beating well after each addition. Beat in the vanilla until just combined.

4. Slowly add the flour mixture, beating until combined. Pour the batter into the prepared pan, smoothing it into an even layer.

5. Bake for 40 minutes or until a wooden pick inserted in the center comes out clean.

6. Let cake cool in the pan on a wire rack for 20 minutes. Carefully remove the cake from the pan, discard the parchment paper, and place it on a serving plate. Serve warm drizzled with 3 tablespoons of honey.

Tip: Mix 1 cup of greek yoghurt with 2 tablespoons of honey. Serve on the side - delicious!

Also by C. A. Phipps

The Maple Lane Cozy Mysteries

Sugar and Sliced - Maple Lane Prequel

Apple Pie and Arsenic

Bagels and Blackmail

Cookies and Chaos

Doughnuts and Disaster

Eclairs and Extortion

Fudge and Frenemies

Gingerbread and Gunshots

Honey Cake and Homicide

Midlife Potions - Paranormal Cozy Mysteries

Witchy Awakening

Witchy Hot Spells

Witchy Flash Back

Witchy Bad Blood

Witchy Coffee Crime - preorder now!

Witches and Wishes Cozy Mysteries

A Wish To Die For - coming soon!

Beagle Diner Cozy Mysteries

Beagles Love Cupcake Crimes

Beagles Love Steak Secrets

Beagles Love Muffin But Murder

Beagles Love Layer Cake Lies

The Cozy Café Mysteries

Sweet Saboteur

Candy Corruption

Mocha Mayhem

Berry Betrayal

Deadly Desserts

Please note: Most are also available in paperback and some in audio.

Remember to join Cheryl's Cozy Mystery newsletter.

There's a free recipe book waiting for you. ;-)

Cheryl also writes romance as Cheryl Phipps.

I couldn't have this wonderful career that I love without the support of Himself and my lovely Beta readers, Suzanne, Linda, Bernie and Barb.

I also want to thank my kind reviewers. What you say does matter and I'm so grateful for you taking the time to help an author.

Cheryl x

About the Author

'Life is a mystery. Let's follow the clues together.'

C. A. Phipps is a USA Today best-selling author from beautiful New Zealand. Cheryl is an empty-nester living in a quiet suburb with her wonderful husband, 'himself'. With an extended family to keep her busy when she's not writing, there is just enough space for a crazy mixed breed dog who stole her heart! She enjoys family times, baking, and her quest for the perfect latte.

Check out her website http://caphipps.com

facebook.com/authorcaphipps

x.com/CherylAPhipps

instagram.com/caphippsauthor

9 798227 832917